STARS BURNING

EXILES: VOLUME THREE

ASHLEY CAPES

Stars Burning

(Exiles: 3)
Copyright © 2023 by Ashley Capes

Cover: Illustration & Design by Vivid Covers
Layout & Typeset: David Schembri Studios

ISBN-978-0-6486237-2-4

www.ashleycapes.com

Published by Close-Up Books
Melbourne, Australia

For the Backers!

CONTENTS

PROLOGUE – CINDER

Cinder drew his borrowed horse, Flip, to a halt near the grand fissure.

Afternoon light plummeted into a gorge cut deep in the earth. The dark opening spanned one edge of the overgrown highway to the other, disappearing within a sparse stand of trees. But it would not be impossible to detour the thing – simply use the plain to circle the fissure and be done with it, delay or no.

A pale mist seemed to be climbing the dark walls, however – a threat? Strangely enough, the mist did seem to be keeping *quite* close to the earth.

He dismounted, approaching at a cautious walk.

So far, not a single *arkedi* had troubled him on the way, nor had he seen any of the Blood Cats... the calm before another storm, perhaps. On the other hand, sand-stalkers did not seem the kind of creatures to plan an ambush. And now, so close to freedom, stolen valuable at his waist, a horse, and even a few provisions in his saddlebag – Denuko's saddlebag, really – was no time to blunder into danger.

At the edge, he leant over to stare down into… more darkness.

No *arkedi* waiting below.

But the white mist was restless, moving without really going anywhere. The longer he stared, the more it seemed the mist was joined by a low, sweet humming. Did the sound align itself with the twirls? It could have been a human voice… or insects… or some great, gentle beast?

Little about the fissure seemed related to the threat of the sand-stalkers, either.

Finally, Cinder shrugged.

Either way, it was time to resume his flight. The Inora did not seem to be under any threat from the gorge, nor the mist. The biggest danger it posed was for some unsuspecting traveller at night.

Cinder strode back toward his horse.

Something caught his foot.

White tendrils of mist. They had slipped up from the very earth, wrapping his ankle – and rising! He fought to wrench his leg free. For all their supposed fragility, the tendrils were all too solid. Another joined the first, and then a third had his other leg.

He cursed as it tugged him to the ground, heart thumping within his chest now.

The knife!

Cinder tore at the blade but even as he drew and slashed at the pale bindings, half a dozen replaced them, dragging him closer and closer to the gorge.

"No!"

But it was no use. The more he cut with the gleaming blade, the more mist appeared. Worse, the tendrils pulled at great speed now, only slowing when his hip smacked into a rock.

He cried out, but it did not stop him; he only bounced closer to the fissure.

By Aehtu, I can't stop them!

And then the earth fell away beneath him, sky receding as he plummeted, reaching hopelessly for the blue.

CHAPTER 1. – MEI

Mei paced the darkened garden while Sorcerer Onolse worked on a cure for the curse and its illness – requiring "not a single interruption" as he had to care for not only his apprentice, but Mamalo and Nata too.

How much time would he need? Could he succeed at all? As capable as Onolse seemed, he didn't have many answers about the curse… *And what if I'm next?*

Mei lifted a hand to her brow. Too warm? And the sweat – was it left over from her flight from the ship? Or the same warning sign that eventually struck down the others? *Probably just because I'm worrying.* Not without cause, however. She glanced back toward the shopfront, where not so long ago Onolse had arranged for another sorcerer to check on Captain Minath. Which was also a risk.

A cry echoed from the street – a shrill note. A child's voice.

Mei charged into the shop, twisting through the shelves, feet pounding across the floorboards. She yanked open the door and leapt outside.

A figure of luminous sand stood within the street.

Like the thing that attacked me and Jeniva!

The creature flowed across the stones, leaving a glittering trail as it approached Onolse's shop, elongated head swivelling. No scales filled its form, just more of the bright sand. Why was it different?

Not important.

Beyond, a child clung to her mother's skirts, eyes wide. The woman stood still, staring up at the sky with rigid arms. And she wasn't the only one; two more citizens were frozen in place, necks craned.

At the feet of one man, a broken bottle spilled dark liquid across the cobblestones – and up and down the street was the echo of footfalls as people fled.

Are any of them alive?

The glow brightened.

"Stop!" Mei shouted at the thing.

Its soft head twitched at her voice, but the creature did not slow – and why would it? *Shouting won't do anything, you fool.* Mei gathered her power, drawing as much strength as she could, not stopping when her temples began to throb.

The sand-creature was too dangerous for anything less than a single, devastating blow.

Shouts of shock echoed around her as yet more people became aware of the threat, but Mei held her ground even as her pulse raced. *A little longer.* Pain was spreading through her skull, darkness threatening the edges of her vision… but she had to be sure.

The strange thing was so close, tiny sparks of gold visible – Mei released the power.

Sand exploded.

Glittering fragments shot across the street, twisting to

hang in the air before floating down in tiny pieces or small clumps. Wherever they touched a surface, stone or timber, cloth or flesh, the sand winked out. Even the large patch at her feet was fading away to nothing.

Mei lowered herself to one knee as exhaustion swept in, but she was still able to smile. *It worked.*

"It certainly did."

A strong voice had spoken familiar words; ones she hadn't heard since leaving Nokema. Mei lifted her head, blinking away the blurred edges.

He's Inora! The man was tall with grey hair and dark stubble on his cheeks, his eyes weary. He wore a black tunic beneath a pale cloak of plain cut, but no garments that would mark him as hailing from Nokema.

Of course, he could not hide his pale complexion. Nor his power.

The sense of a vast and furious strength was clear, tempered by… determination? Or was it regret? While she could not decide what it was exactly, one thing was very clear. This man was as strong – or perhaps stronger – than Iggy.

"Who are you?"

He extended a gloved hand, as if to help her up but Mei did not reach for it.

A faint smile passed his lips. "Thorn."

She met his gaze, which was unwavering, and he did not elaborate. No-one from the village would name a child such a thing – all were derived from names of the parents, and theirs before.

"I do not recognise you," she said. Which meant he was an Outcast or an Exile… or… was he perhaps actually from

Senoja? Was it just her earring that made it seem like his Senoja words were familiar Nokema ones? *That doesn't seem quite right.*

"Nor should you, Meiaja."

Mei tried to gather what was left of her gift, but even the thought of striking out with her mind caused her to wilt.

The man who called himself Thorn knelt beside her. "Stay conscious if you can, otherwise I will have to carry you."

But she could not.

CHAPTER 2. – IGGY

The sun's rays touched everything; they were absolutely and utterly everywhere.

And all at once, too.

Iggy had only to follow one brilliant thread to… anywhere, really. Far easier than he'd ever imagined, such was the power of the sun. When it rose, it covered the entire land, and so long as he did not aim for the shadows, he could arrive at a place within a blink.

A place he had already visited, at least.

Or, if the need is great enough, to the side of a person I know, thankfully.

Which meant that, once he had a face, it would be time to check on Mei…

So it was that he stumbled back through the hole he had made in the giant log, back into darkness where the Mistress of Obsidian waited, his bloody hand still clutching the box rescued from the Nasaru.

And before he strode further, he turned, as if to see Rokura… *You'd better be alive, old man.*

Iggy's soft footfalls hit black tiles for a mere handful of

paces before he stopped, where the enormous petal throne awaited, where the Mistress sat, legs crossed at the ankles as she smiled down at him.

"I see your task was both simpler and more dangerous than I imagined." Her deep voice filled the space, not quite a 'sound' as Mei had described them to him in the past, something difficult to understand, but somehow still comforting in its firmness.

It was.

"Your success is welcome, nevertheless."

Did you know the Nasaru had already retrieved it?

"Only that they were close, which is why I asked you to intervene – whether that ended up being before *or* after it was freed from the shipwreck."

Just how powerful was she? *You knew we were approaching?*

"I called to you from afar – with help from Nuka."

One hand drifted up to the tooth that hung upon a simple leather necklace he'd made. Maybe not a surprise, after all.

"Once you left the Valley, we were seeking you, Iggy."

We? You and Nuka.

"Yes."

The Mistress did not elaborate, and Nuka remained silent, as so often she had in the past… unless it came to information about how he might reach the Mistress. That she had been happy to parcel out.

Iggy glanced down at the velvet box, somehow free of waterstains and decay, but not blood from where Edazol's blade had cut his forearm. *How will you use this to gain your freedom?*

Inside waited another being. Something like Nuka and the Mistress herself, that much was clear from the moment he held it, but what did that mean? Death and destruction, as Rokura feared?

"*Our* freedom."

Iggy glanced up to her dark eyes. *Who have I carried here?*

"My other sister. Come, if you wish for me to uphold my end of our bargain, lay them both before me."

He knelt to place the box near her feet, each of her toes larger than his whole palm, then opened the lid. It swung on smooth hinges to reveal a skeletal-hand, knuckle bones a bright, clean white.

Next, Iggy removed the necklace where Nuka hung.

Itula will wake soon, Nuka said. *Thank you, Iggy. You're a clever boy.*

He stepped back.

The Mistress was changing; darkening upon her throne, shades draining until only grey remained. And upon the bed of now-brittle petals, a black ribcage… yet it was not giant, not even human-sized, but smaller.

And the other bones were shrinking too!

What is happening?

Iggy received no answer, but the air shimmered above each item… wavering figures of light. Like flames – one pale, one grey and the other darker still – each appearing roughly human in shape.

Their voices rang in his mind, as distinct as their flames.

Now *this* is freedom. And after so long trapped in a box, even a velvet box, I cannot quite believe just how lovely this feels.

The first voice came from the grey spirit; Itula sounded younger than the others.

Nuka reached out and so did the Mistress, the shades joining in an embrace, joyous laughter echoing about the darkness.

What about our saviour? Itula asked. Will he be enough?

Of course, Nuka replied.

Enough for what? Iggy focused on the Mistress. *Are you planning to betray me, after all?*

She floated forward to envelope him – from without *and* within. As though she was pushing through his skin and tendons, hot against his very bones. The range of his awareness crumbled to nothing.

Know that I have never broken a promise.

Other shades joined her within his body, bringing cold and a stinging pain that charged along his veins, most viscous at the cut in his arm. Altogether, the assault on his senses was too much. It drove Iggy to his knees, a scream ringing within his mind.

And then a pure hush replaced the chaos.

He fell back, stretching out across the smooth tiles, chest heaving… a strange heaviness within his torso. A faint glow drew his attention. Three symbols were fading into his skin – a tooth, a hand, and ribcage.

The bones no longer rested before him.

He sat upright.

What did you do?

In order to return to life – and to grant you a face as you desire – we have joined you.

He slapped the tiles with both hands. It had been the Mistress, but her voice echoed from within his mind. *You did not mention this!*

Yet it must be so. My power, combined with that of my sisters, is the only thing that will offer success.

You lied.

No, she didn't, sweet Iggy, **Nuka said softly**. It will take the four of us to drain Kaziuu, the Moon Father. Once we do that, we can live again and you will have a face. We promise.

We promise. Itula, this time, and it seemed she could have been grinning. Trust us.

No! You all need to leave.

The Mistress sighed, impatience clear in her words. **You must adapt. It cannot be undone until we face Kaziuu, in any event.**

Must I? He stood and stormed off toward the exit, yet for no other reason than to be able to stamp his feet, perhaps. *Clearly, I have no choice.*

No, you do not.

CHAPTER 3. – IGGY

According to the sisters, who could recede in and out of his consciousness at will, returning to Malkaha Marsh before nightfall had put him within fair distance of reaching first Senoja, and then the resting place of the mysterious Kaziuu.

Or, at least *a* resting place for the one they called Moon Father.

But as Iggy trudged along the barren edges of the marsh, feet sinking into the soft earth as often as not, something else weighed upon his mind. Something Nuka had revealed.

Mei had travelled west.

Mei had travelled west, thinking she was following him.

Still trying to protect me.

He shook his head, both in regret and frustration. What a risk she'd taken! Yet, wasn't it just like his own risk? Even so, if she followed, and was hurt or worse, then such a thing… it wasn't right. *I ran to ease your suffering, Mei, don't you know that?*

But she could not answer, of course. And all Nuka had been able to reveal was that a young woman 'just like him' travelled the marsh and turned west, weeks ago now.

The Mistress did not offer her own insights, nor did Itula,

who was the most quiet of the three… or perhaps the most secretive. Only sometimes did they speak amongst themselves, their voices pleasant enough, but theirs was a language he could not fathom. That alone was unusual, since he never really had to understand languages so much as *thoughts*.

And whenever they did converse, their words interfered with his thoughts.

Sometimes, even his limbs…

A test? Or accident?

There was no-one he could ask. Not without alerting the sisters to the fact that he'd realised *something* was happening.

When finally Iggy reached the banks of a stream, his strength holding up well enough under the fading sunlight, he dunked his head to drink. Cool water seeped through his skin and quenched his thirst.

He sat back then, cross-legged upon the ground. Water dripped from his hair and onto his shoulders, down the front of his tunic too. It was not so wet that his clothing would need to be dried out, but lowering his chin to check *did* offer another reminder: change had not only occurred within his mind.

The three markings were, for now, hidden beneath fabric – dark symbols somehow burnt into his skin without pain, three familiar shapes. *One for each of you.*

They will not fade once our work is complete – but they are beautiful, are they not?

He did not respond to what the Mistress had told him. Instead, his question was about Mei. *Is Mei in danger right now?*

For the moment she is not.

What does that mean?

She is being deceived by the one she travels with, that much I can sense. Nuka? Itula?

I can only agree.

I see another from Nokema... older. Itula seemed troubled.

Is that all you can tell me? Where is she, exactly?

Senoja.

And then the sisters faded, becoming a mere hint of voices, or a vague impression of their shades. Iggy sighed as he crawled toward a thicket of trees bearing dark leaves, settling in to wrap himself within the old cloak Rokura had made for him.

How long ago that seemed now. Yet it had been less than a day since he'd woken in their room, only to find Rokura gone, having to race to the man's side at the wharves.

You know, I helped you then. Itula did not sound angry, so much as proud. Without my call, you wouldn't have woken in time.

He did not thank her, did not respond at all.

Let him sleep, sister.

Of course.

Nuka spoke last, her voice merely a whisper. We will watch over you, Iggy.

***

It was a long time before they spoke again.

The next morning, the sisters gave him directions as he reached a swift river, crossing courtesy of an old bridge, but then nothing more until nightfall. Unlike before, he now collected bare, fragmentary impressions of the conversations they carried in their secret language, but nothing of use.

Each day passed in a similar fashion as he drew closer to the border: he kept away from travellers, merchants and towns and villages alike, stopping of a night to conceal himself wherever possible, asking the sisters about Mei and learning little of her location. Asking sometimes of the Moon Father.

The things Iggy did learn about Kaziuu's plan to smother the land and people in bright sands, and the sky in endless darkness, those were bad enough, but just as troubling was what the sisters expected of him.

Kaziuu would be confronted directly.

Supposedly, the sisters would drain the Moon Father's vast power but beyond that claim, they had nothing that resembled a strategy.

Neither do you. The thought was his own, but it could have been spoken by Rokura. *Well said.* Would the man also have considered himself vindicated regarding his initial distrust of Nuka? To describe hosting three… ghosts… as unexpected was quite the understatement.

But what had I thought would happen?

Death, perhaps.

Death had seemed the only certainty in the world beyond the Valley, and being buried had nearly proved his expectations. But he pushed the jumbled memories away – or was it more that they were simply too jagged? Too painful.

A bitter spark had somehow helped him cling to life.

To defiance.

After being rescued, an actual desire came to the fore – to be made complete, to be given a face. But now he had to find Mei too, to be sure she was safe. *Just like she tried to do for me.*

For who else would have followed after his Exile? No-one.

More days passed in the tedium of travel and he pushed his body on, striking out beneath the blessings of sunlight, carrying water when he could not find a river or stream, guided by the sisters when it seemed he might not find more. Until finally, *finally*, he reached the feet of the Senoja mountains.

Stone rose higher and darker than the Dalma Ranges, its sides covered in dark pine trees and narrower, greyer saplings he did not recognise. No hint of a mountain pass or cave system to travel beneath, just a wall. *We're too far from the border. There's no pass.*

Leave that to us. The Mistress sounded as though she smiled, and she did not elaborate. She *did* murmur a few words to her sisters, once more speaking in their own tongue. It was tantalisingly familiar, but no matter how closely he listened, he could not fathom anything other than an immeasurable age to the words, a *rightness* to them.

Iggy folded his arms. *Keeping secrets from me while I carry you around is not appreciated.*

Patience, boy. We are going to carry you across the mountains, yet you complain?

He flinched at the sharpness to her tone, Rokura's stories of her wrath returning. And more, she seemed to be waiting for an apology.

I'm sorry. I'm worried about Mei.

Regarding your sister, there is little time to waste.

Why?

Kaziuu is close to waking and it seems she is an unwitting part of that – it is a matter of weeks or days, and we cannot wait while you cross the range by conventional means. There is, however, a cost you must pay.

He straightened. *Fine. What cost?*

Afterward, you will not be able to move. But you should survive.

We are reasonably sure of that. And when you recover, you will be as strong as ever, in mind and body.

I should *survive?*

Itula chuckled. You're made of stronger stuff than you imagine. We are rarely incorrect, dear.

That's not comforting. Iggy strode from the mountains, feet stirring dust as he angled toward a small stand of trees. A fallen log waited at its edge, a suitable enough place to sit a moment, and perhaps even sun-bathe to restore some strength.

But the moment he slumped down, the Mistress was urging him back to his feet – yet he did not rise. Not until he was given more answers. *I need you to explain what will happen.*

It is not simple to describe. We will fly you across the mountains, for as long as your body can withstand straddling the line between corporeal and incorporeal. It is not so dissimilar to how you travel via the sun's rays.

But there is a difference that makes it dangerous, isn't there?

As forewarned, yes. The difference is that you will be passing through shadow, as we can. That will come at a cost to an Inora, especially one so powerful as you.

I see. Despite her words, it was actually better to be given information for a change. At least that way, making a decision could be based on at least some small understanding of the risk. *And it is the only way to reach Mei in time?*

No-one could traverse the range fast enough without either your power or ours.

And it cannot happen until nightfall?

Correct.

He removed his tunic, then stretched out and closed his eyes, letting the sunlight sink into his skin; a welcome thing, a beautiful thing. *Let me think, Mistress — at least until it grows dark.*

Of course.

CHAPTER 4. – MEI

Thorn introduced it as the City of Rope but its name was actually Kaarsi – a place within Senoja itself, a place several *days* across the border.

At first, she had not believed her captor when he explained.

She'd woken to find herself tied across the saddle of his packhorse, every thud in the road sending a jolt through her skull. Mei had struggled to even put the world back together in her vision – the blue, green and sparkling white were all a blur.

But Thorn had not untied her until entering what he called a 'rainforest'. There, he dismounted and then helped Mei down and took her to a hunk of rock where it protruded from a wall of moss. Rich green leaves and huge fern trees stood everywhere, their fronds spreading to cast shade across the moss-covered road. A coolness filled the air – likely from the waterfalls that tumbled toward the city.

"You are lying," she'd said upon hearing his description of Kaarsi.

Thorn only shrugged as he checked upon the horses, adjusting the straps beneath his saddle. "The City of Rope itself will change your mind soon enough."

She glared at his back. Was escape possible? *Was I really exhausted, or did he keep me unconscious? I feel good, if not wonderful.* No matter where they were, she could always run… at the right moment. For the sense of his power was unchanged. *Like a hammer hurtling down – but one that never actually hits.* It was an unspoken threat, so that when he faced her once more there was something in his gaze that suggested he knew she was thinking of escape, but considered it such an impossibility that he need not speak any warning.

He hasn't even taken Father's blade.

Who was Thorn? *Nothing about him matches the description of Exiles I know about.* Nor was he so old that *no-one* in the village would have spoken of him… *He doesn't look like the way I remember Dieg.* She shivered. Nor did he appear anything like the monster Pedija, thankfully.

His arrival directly after the sand-creature was clearly suspicious.

Whatever his true identity, Thorn could not be allowed to continue to believe he held the upper hand at every turn – true or not.

Mei had stood then, and strode back to the pack horse, where she climbed into the saddle, using the stirrup and holding the reins as Mamalo had taught her. Then, she stared down at Thorn. "Why have you brought me here?"

A flicker of confusion crossed his face, before he answered. "I need a lure."

"A lure?" She frowned at him, in part to smother another shiver. "Why?"

"In the city."

And though she asked again, he did not answer as he led them down the slope, accompanied by the soft roar of the waterfall, something that was only half-glimpsed via sparkling white through the leaves.

He did not bother to bind her, nor did he keep a close watch on the lead rope to her mount. *Does he want me to try escaping?* Just like being captured by Anyo, but still unlikely. And what did Thorn mean by lure? *Is he trying to say… that I attract the sand-things? That doesn't seem right either.*

She glanced over her shoulder to the shaded back-trail; an empty highway. Four days to the border… how nice to imagine that if she fled that way, Mamalo, Nilo and Nata would be there, following to rescue her.

If they really have survived…

Thorn's voice sounded amused. "You can hardly see so far."

"What?"

"You are looking over your shoulder, as if you could see all the way back to your friends," he replied. "They might even have recovered; Onolse has a sterling reputation."

Mei did not answer. *Is he reading my mind, or just my bearing?* She did not speak again until they neared a valley floor, where the highway spread into a wide clearing – still paved – the ferns now so tall and wide that their bases were like dark, furry walls.

There, Thorn dismounted and removed travel rations from his pack, offering her golden hard-bread and water. She dismounted herself this time, accepting the food and taking a bite… and the flavour bore traces of familiar spices.

"Where did you find this?" she asked, the words slipping out. *Pajen-bread. Just like back home.* Such a simple reminder of the village, but the comfort was heavy with bitterness.

He continued to eat in silence.

Her next bite had her gnashing her teeth a moment before taking a breath. Whether he liked it or not, she would pry something useful out of the man. "What was the thing I destroyed?"

"A Grain of the Moon Father."

Few of the words in his response offered anything familiar.

He continued his explanation after noting her expression, which was obviously enough for him to expand. "The Grains have various names: Children, Pale-Walkers, Sand-Wraiths – choose as you see fit."

"That doesn't tell me anything. What had they done to those people? Why did one attack me in the Valley, and in the street?"

"Grains naturally seek out the strong ones. We are targets for them."

"We? The Inora?"

He nodded. "For obvious reasons."

"Meaning?"

Thorn frowned. "That you should know why, of course. Or have the Paragons shared nothing?"

"About what? The Moon Father and his so-called Grains?"

"Yes."

"I have never once heard such words from *anyone* in the village."

The man's eyes widened a little. "And they call themselves Guardians. I knew it was bad, but I hadn't thought it like this."

"What do you mean by that, Thorn?"

He shook his head, then shrugged. "Very well. The Moon

Father is an old terror seeking a dark rule, but a terror which has long been sealed beyond the Moon Gate. As the Seal weakens, grains of his lunar sand – in some tongues, his Children, spread across the lands seeking food, slaves and of course, Guardians to attack, be they Nokema or the few remaining in Senoja. At first, their strength will not be of true concern. At first."

His explanation was now no longer difficult to understand… but difficult to believe. Or at least, it should have been. *But I've seen them with my own eyes.* Were such things really working under the directive of some long-forgotten power sealed within the Moon Gate?

What of the vast pressure she'd felt while passing through the mountain? A force Jeniva had not considered so troubling. *But it was worse for me.* "If what you say is true, why aren't we guarding the place? I cannot believe Nokema would forget, not even after generations."

"Nor could I."

Mei pointed at him. "You do not share your true name, nor your purpose. Why should I consider your words anything more than fanciful at best, or lies at the worst?"

"Convince yourself however you must," he replied.

Mei met his gaze, once again unable to pierce his expression to learn anything of value about the man who called himself Thorn. A different question, then. One she'd already asked, but one she needed to know the answer to if she was ever to escape. "Why bring me here?"

"I have said as much – as a lure."

"For *what?*" she snapped.

He sighed. "For your brother."

Mei lowered her meal. "You know where Iggy is?"

"I will," he said as he tossed the near-burnt crust into the undergrowth, then gestured to her mount. "Save your questions until we reach the city – I need some peace."

CHAPTER 5. – MEI

Somehow, Thorn actually stopped her speaking before and during their approach to Kaarsi, and though she railed against whatever he had done, despite her glares, it made no difference. Unlike anything anyone at home had ever demonstrated, the power of his mind was enough to prevent her speaking a single word.

She had to follow his horse across the small plain and its trails of moss and flowers, passing no-one resting or travelling from the city, nor from distant farms, just blue butterflies and puddles filled with clouds.

That, and the reflected image of the City of Rope.

The place was enough to guarantee her silence with or without Thorn's power.

Somehow, the city was surrounded by a moat of rope. It stretched on and on and on around the city... and moving steadily along those ropes were huge baskets carrying people. *Why?* The bridge that led into Kaarsi had been lowered, supported by more rope – enormous, twined bolts so large that each strand was the width of a carriage.

Not even a giant could have made such a thing.

The stone walls themselves bore patterns of rope too. *Are they obsessed with it here?* She might have asked Thorn, but even if she could speak, would he have answered? Mei had already tried and failed to send thoughts to him, proving equally futile.

When crossing the bridge, she glanced down to the passenger baskets. The nearest revealed a handful of people dressed in bright colours, their faces unclear from the distance, but their manner seeming unconcerned, as if such a thing was utterly normal.

Which it is, for them.

There was no delay at the gates. Barely glanced over by the guards, one of whom Thorn greeted cheerfully. She found herself inside, head swivelling at more wonders. For while the buildings were of stone and wood with round windows, Kaarsi truly was the city of rope first and foremost.

Above, stretching from building to building, more rope with baskets. All just as sturdy-looking as those on the outside. Inside, however, such baskets moved between the taller buildings quite quickly. The supports were connected to huge steel rings that slid along the rope with a muted rasp – many of the lines angled downward to create speed.

Even as she watched, men dressed in black trousers and pale vests appeared upon one of the rooftops. Without pause, they worked a large wheel that seemed to lower the endpoint of the rope. For crossing *from* the building opposite?

It seemed that basket-riders could choose which storey they wanted to land on, based on the regular platforms and the wheel.

"Curious?" Thorn asked.

Since she could not speak, she merely nodded.

"I admit, even I admired the city's ropes, at first. It's not a method without flaws, since accidents do happen, but it is interesting. You might get to use one yourself, before we leave."

He kept them to one side of the street, passing through crowds of people wearing a mix of coats, tunics and sometimes short pants that revealed sandals upon their feet, calling to one another from across the streets or from the round windows, which brought Jeniva's ship to mind.

Thorn soon stopped where a sluggish river split the city in half.

From where she sat, the streets and buildings opposite were no different – nor the people. Besides which, she was still staring up at the rope-baskets flying overhead, these crossing the river in regular intervals. Some baskets were smaller than she'd seen so far, carrying one or two people, but most were able to support four or five... the rope was obviously *very* strong.

"We will be taking a more uninspiring path to my inn," Thorn said as he brought his horse to a halt before a bridge with multiple arches. It spanned the river but at three points across, the walkway expanded into a wide circle. There, people stopped to talk, to purchase food from merchants in... standing tents?

Some citizens had even stopped to listen to a small group of musicians, while others stood to wave at those few boats she saw, oars making no sound at such a distance.

Mei opened her mouth to answer Thorn – and she was actually able to speak for a change. "And then?"

"I teach you what you need to know to call your brother, how to better protect yourself against the Grains, and above all, more about the Moon Father."

"You're assuming I'm going to help you."

"You want to see your brother. He is finally in Senoja; I sense him now."

Mei clenched a hand. "You can't manipulate me like that – or Iggy."

"Yet I must and will," he said with a sigh. "You will call him and he will come, and together, we will destroy the Moon Father. It is in your nature; you won't stand by and let others suffer, Mei."

"Don't pretend to know what I would choose."

"Whatever you decide, you must accompany me to The Guardian now. And not only because you are alone in an unfamiliar land, and not only because I could find you in mere moments if you run, but because, as I have said, you want to find your brother. You need to know he is well, and you need to protect him. And you cannot do that from afar, Mei."

"I can go to him."

"Can you? Where is he?"

She glared at Thorn; his calm demeanour made everything worse. And of course he was right. *But that doesn't change anything.*

"Do not discount the Grains. Some will be able to find you just as easily as I can." His expression changed enough to permit a little sadness. "Think back. How would you have fared against two or three? I saved you for a reason bigger than either of us."

"But you didn't ask," she said, her voice raised now.

Onlookers had started to give them a wide berth.

"I admit to a necessary cruelty." Thorn's reply was hardly an apology and not much of an admission, either. "But I will not let this chance pass me by. I have waited and watched for far too long. Now follow me, Mei of Nokema, and I will show you to your room."

CHAPTER 6. – NILO

Nilo frowned down at the mud. Some of it had reached his sleeves since he hadn't rolled them up enough and the trench beside the road was too deep by far. *And I can hardly clean them properly on the road – how are people meant to take me seriously looking like this?* "Would anyone like to help?"

Nata snorted. "You dropped it."

Nilo glanced to Mamalo, but the merchant was feeding his horse from an oat bag, his back turned. The man, for all his impatience, was taking the delay well enough. On the other hand, whoever had abducted Mei was obviously heading to the City of Rope, and the substitute mirror suggested as much too.

With only one road through the beautiful green of the rainforest, the trail was obvious.

His fingers closed around something hard and he drew it forth with a grin.

Just a smooth shard of stone.

"Are you sure about this, Alo?" Nata asked.

"Of course," Mamalo replied. "We owe her our lives as much as we do Onolse, for one thing."

Nilo clenched his teeth as he stretched deeper into the ditch, yet still no luck – only more mud.

"That the only reason?"

The merchant exhaled. "Are you asking me if I want to rescue Mei from whoever has taken her for selfish reasons that relate to my desire to trade illicit goods?"

"Yes."

Nilo glanced at Mamalo as he shifted his arms, hands finally brushing against a hard, smooth edge – the mirror at last! He pulled it free in time to see Mamalo shake his head.

"That is no secret. But contrary to what you may or may not believe, I do feel responsibility toward her. Further, your reasons are, I'm sure, entirely taken in regard to Mei's safety and not your own orders, loyal foot-soldier of King Mutolo that you are."

Nata's lips became a hard line. "Insults?"

"And your tactless question was what, exactly?" Mamalo asked. "It's obvious we all have various reasons for taking this risk."

"Found it," Nilo announced, before Nata could answer – and it seemed she had been about to snap back with some venom. Why so much friction between the two? Something to do with how or why Mamalo left the king's service? *This had better not get me killed somehow, somewhere along the way.*

It was very much a dangerous path they were treading. Not just visiting Senoja lands, that was always a risk for a citizen of either nation who crossed the border, but because a merchant, Greyshield, and sorcerer travelling together would draw all kinds of unwanted attention.

Deciding to essentially dispense with any attempt at

subterfuge and instead shouting out their relative strength was almost a bluff, but it would also deter interference from some and cause others to approach with caution. *Hopefully.*

"Fitting that you recovered the mirror, since you were the one to drop it in the first place," Nata muttered to him.

Nilo narrowed his eyes. "My dear, let's not forget who was responsible for our swift passage through the Senoja border."

Mamalo burst into a bitter laugh as he ran a hand through his hair. "Isn't this wonderful? If only we could send Mei a message to let her know that she need not worry, no matter what she's suffering, because three imbeciles who cannot put aside their differences are stuck arguing over a puddle of mud."

In the heavy silence that followed, Nata raised her hands. "You're right."

Nilo nodded. "This seems as good a time as any to press on. Kaarsi is less than an hour by now, even by carriage."

"Strange that we haven't seen many merchants or others passing by," Mamalo said as he climbed up to the driver's seat. "Even with trade so heavily regulated."

Nata swung into her own saddle. "There have been whispers of something amiss but little in the way of specifics and none of them verified."

"Between the three of us, I trust we will be on the lookout for surprises," Nilo said as he set the mirror down and then splashed some of his water across it, cleaning it as best he could.

"Surprises are called so for a reason," Mamalo said as he snapped his reins. "But I do agree with your sentiment. Let's get going."

Nilo followed, letting his horse do most of the work as they made their descent toward the City of Rope, still hidden beyond the mighty ferns. While talk of motives lingered in his mind, it was hard not to turn his thoughts to Mei's captor.

According to the substitute Mirror of the Sky, whoever had taken her was able to conceal himself. Even where he rode beside her, the man's face and body remained unclear, as if hidden. And despite glimpses of boots and once a gloved hand, there was nothing to reveal the identity of the captor, let alone purpose of their actions.

Yet *something* had slipped free of his defences.

I know this man, somehow. He might have been a customer...

Such a claim was, of course, not at all worth sharing. At least, not until some certainty had been gained. Familiarity with the abductor remained unpleasant, at best. Perhaps most troubling was the stirring within his very veins, an excitement that could only come from the danger inherent to their task. Like visiting *and returning* from the Raging Isle. *Or saving Master.*

Granted, the sea-sickness had not been much of a thrill.

Nor the near-death experience courtesy of the Black Sand's curse – the feverish nightmares themselves far worse than the crippling aches of recovery, and especially true considering the relative ease with which the aches passed.

Alas, the same could not be said for the nightmares.

He glanced at the others. *At least I'm not the only one waking in a sweat each night, heart thundering within my chest.* Somehow, the shared burden made dealing with the terror a *little* better.

Onolse had not been able to estimate when or if the harrowing dreams would end, but physically he had declared them all recovered. Nor would the man give up on his experiments with the Black Sand, dangerous as it was. Far too dangerous to take along on a rescue-attempt.

Even so, that power…

In the short time he'd worked with the Black Sand to craft Mei's mirror, the vast potential had been obvious. Not enough for him to estimate the bounds, but the thrill had not worn away, not even days later.

"Nilo, what do you think?"

He glanced up from the mirror.

Nata was looking across at him. "Forgive me, but I admit to being wrapped within my own thoughts."

"Clearly," she said with a small smile. "We've been talking about Mei's captor."

"Guessing at his or her identity again? I admit I've not had much luck."

"His purpose," Mamalo replied. "Taking Mei to Senoja suggests there is someone or something there that wants to use her power."

"We've considered as much."

"Right. Her captor knows that Mei is Inora and expects to be able to conceal her within the land of her ancestors, but what if it goes further? What if they wanted to use her as some sort of rallying point?"

"Interesting," Nilo said. "We have no evidence either way, so why not? But if that is the case, a rallying point for what? An attack on Nasaru?"

Nata lifted her flask to drink before she spoke. "That's what we have to discover, if it's true."

"I'm still wondering about gaining access to the city," Mamalo said. "It has been five or six years since I set foot within the City of Rope; since before that atrocity in the northern villages."

"Are you having doubts?" Nata asked.

"Some. We're going to stand out, no matter how we dress."

"Which is part of why we decided to use our respective roles as a shield – people will see what we are but not dare challenge us. At least, not low-ranking guards and citizens. They'll assume we have the necessary trade passes. Either that, or we have you wear grey too, and they think we're a diplomatic envoy. I can forge something that will fool most."

He shrugged. "And they'll still assume we are spies."

"People will think that whatever we choose," she replied. "We've been over this."

Nilo was nodding along. "Better to intimidate at least some of those who might impede our search."

The merchant began to massage his temples. "Either way, few will offer us *help*. I'm wondering if that's a bigger problem."

"A fair point." Nata gave him a look. "Since you're the only one who has actually entered the City of Rope, do you have any ideas?"

"I do," he said with a shrug. "It poses a risk, like all of our options, but there is one group that is generally welcome anywhere, a group that passes borders easily enough."

"Travelling entertainers? Perhaps in the past…"

"No. I mean the Fiodan."

She nodded slowly. "Of course. But aren't they… well, not exactly… stable?"

"I travelled with a pair once," he replied. "They had some odd ideas, but they were not that bad. Just religious clerics, when you get right down to it."

"Well…"

"Trust me," Mamalo said. "They offer healing to any and all and so they're always welcome, seen as harmless and never considered targets, right?"

"That is true, yes."

Nilo cleared his throat. "Aren't you both forgetting something? It won't be that easy to impersonate them – what if someone asks us for treatment?"

The merchant grinned. "That's where you come in, my sorcerer-friend."

CHAPTER 7. – ANYO

Ebatru had grown more impressive – in a limited manner – since Anyo last saw his brother.

Even more a wall of muscles, the man's breastplate remained immaculate, Royal Wings engraved and Black Coral swirling where it had been set within steel bracers, visible when he lifted a hand to point. His face might have been handsome, save for a twist that came only from a lifetime of looking down upon others. "Answer me, little brother. What are you doing here?"

Ebatru's voice was just a little higher than might be expected, something he had always been somewhat self-conscious about. *And something Chioatta and I would tease him over in our more childish moments.*

"Crossing the mountains."

"I see." He rested a hand upon the heavy mace he carried. "That is to say, crossing the border. And with foreign... dignitaries, are they?" The man's gaze moved to Nuvin and Binya, especially.

"If that helps you grant us passage."

His expression denigrated to something of a leer. "Still

begging, I see, brother."

Anyo started forward but something stopped him – Han caught his shoulder. "Careful, lad."

"Very diplomatic of you, Hanibalo." Ebatru gestured to his men, having them fan out but not advance. And not, as yet, draw. But all were ready with sword or bow, and the sorcerers could have been concealing any number of abilities. They likely would have drank or imbued weapons or items prior to the chase.

"Your Highness, you know we pose no threat to the kingdom," Han said.

"His pathetic little search?" The prince laughed. "Of course not. Why Father ever tolerated such nonsense from one of his sons, I'll never know."

"If such nonsense is so far beneath you, we'll be on our way," Anyo said.

"What is beneath me, is a brother like yourself! That you would beg for the life of some common Takirov? It stains me still. And worst of all, little Anyo – you fancy yourself king one day." Ebatru spat. "I'd rather see that bitch Kiteka get it."

Anyo made a fist. "That man did nothing wrong."

"Meaning what? You defied Father and the nation for some filthy worm."

Defying Father had been nothing – perhaps even a pleasure at the time. More, it had been the right thing to do. And no words from Ebatru would change that now. *He's jealous and paranoid – and I don't actually* need *the throne to change Nasaru.* Anyo unclenched his hand. "And now I am leaving. I pose no threat to your ambitions."

"You still think me a fool?" Ebatru waved an arm with a

shrug. "Take them."

Shrill cries burst overhead.

A shower of wings and flashing beaks fell upon Ebatru and his men. Birds of all shapes and sizes swooped, screeched, and tore at them, chaos following.

"Quickly," Nuvin shouted, already halfway to the steel carriage.

Anyo charged after.

Ebatru's shouts of fury echoed but it seemed the birds were doing their job – an arrow flashed by to bounce off the carriage. Anyo didn't stop but caught a glimpse of blood on the arrow head as he leapt inside. The clank of the lever being slammed down had the Sky Carriage moving, lurching forward. Binya was right behind, arms outstretched. He caught her, pulling her inside and they hit the carriage floor with a grunt.

Binya grinned down at him, her face quite close to his own. "I'm not that heavy, you know."

Katonga was reaching over to slam the door closed.

Another arrow clinked against the window, but barely seemed to trouble the glass as the Sky Carriage slid from the clearing.

Below, most of Ebatru's force had scattered, still hounded by sharp talons and beaks. Ebatru himself was nowhere to be seen, but one of the Coral Sorcerers stood with arms raised, a ball of flame spinning between his hands.

What new terror is this?

Something small dashed from the trees to latch onto the man's leg – a fox! The sorcerer flinched and the ball of fire sputtered out.

And then the Sky Carriage passed up and beyond the reach of his brother and the clearing.

"What was that?" Binya asked.

Anyo sat up, leaning against the door, since the seats had been taken. "The sorcerer or the attack? The birds were Nuvin, right?"

"Indeed," the man replied from where he sat beside his sisters. His eyes were troubled. "Though I worry about the cost; I may have severely eroded trust of the animals, now. They did not wish to come."

"Oh." Troubling as that was, the ball of fire was an equal concern. Exactly what had Ebatru been up to at the border? Few Coral Sorcerers were able to create such things, surely?

Katonga was peering back, as best he could. "We'll have to do the watching ourselves for a while."

"Expecting pursuit?" Han asked.

"It's possible."

Anyo nodded, though he could not be sure. There had been a second carriage… but was Ebatru's pride hurt enough to care?

"Let's not forget whatever stacked those bodies back there," Binya added.

"True." Anyo closed his eyes a moment. If the gods could arrange just a single moment of respite before facing another threat…

"Did you cut your arm?" Binya asked him.

He opened his eyes and there, blood had soaked into his sleeve. *From the arrow?* The sting only now became apparent and he sighed. "Do we have any bandages?"

***

Anyo stared down into the gorge below, where oval patterns of green leaves and orange flowers seemed to return his gaze, swaying slightly in the breeze. The wind was not enough to rock the Sky Carriage, but seated across from him, Nuvin was holding the edge of the seat a little tightly.

Unlike his sisters, Nuvin was not relishing their ascent – and it was not just whatever troubled him about his bond with the birds; he obviously did not care for heights. Both Elin and Fiana, however, had spent most of the journey pressed up against the windows, yet to take much of a turn seated upon the cold carriage floor.

Even now, Elin leant across Anyo, pressing into his shoulder so she could see. Up close, her smiling face did bring a little joy to what was a tense journey. "This really does feel as though we're flying through the sky, doesn't it?"

"A little," he replied with a smile. "Do you want to switch seats?"

"This is fine," she said. "But look. I'm wondering about the orange blossoms down there. Do the patterns that they grow in seem strange to you?"

He followed her gaze and in some parts, the oval shapes were somewhat… interrupted, if nothing else. "A little."

"It's another one," Han said from across the carriage.

Elin shifted and there, visible through the fore window, a motionless Sky Carriage waited upon the opposite cable. And the nearer they drew, the more concerning it became… One door was ripped from its hinges to hang, and both the outside and inside stood covered in dark stains.

"Stop a moment," Anyo said.

Kat pulled the lever and their Sky Carriage slid to a smooth halt, hanging above the gorge directly across from the other carriage, one that would not be finishing its journey.

Inside, remnants of corpses lay frozen beneath the same

grey material from the clearing. Some bodies were little more than a leg or torso; between seat and floor on one side, a head with a missing eye was stuck fast.

Glimpses of Nasaru armour revealed a crest of Royal Wings, the design a little broader than that which was worn today. "The clearing party."

Silence filled the carriage.

"We should keep moving," Han eventually said.

Katonga pulled the handle, and once more the Sky Carriage continued, sliding along the mighty cable with little resistance and a steady pace that defied the angle of ascent.

And so it continued through the sky as they neared one of the peaks, sunlight soon blocked by rising walls of stone. The tops were scattered with jagged points and skeletal remains of shrubs and even, in places, dark openings that might have housed bats or birds, based on the concentration of droppings.

Yet Nuvin did not offer any comment, bearded face still troubled. His sisters no longer stared down and around with traces of wonder or curiosity. No-one had spoken much at all – not until Katonga slowed the carriage again, and Han muttered a string of curses.

Though entirely expected, Anyo found himself glaring ahead at the sealed gate where it stood in the rock-face. The carriage had now come to a final halt, close enough to reach out and touch the stone gate. It was a shallow but protruding dome, carved to resemble a giant eye and it stared back at them, iris shot through with granite.

"Now is the time for brilliant ideas, if any have them to share," he said.

But his answer did not come from the carriage.

Instead, from the gorge below echoed a deep crooning sound that could not at all be considered human.

CHAPTER 8. – ANYO

The crooning grew louder.

Orange blossoms rustled upon the trees below…

Anyo gripped his blade. "It's down there." The pattern was broken as *something* crossed the treetops, and despite the significant drop, the sound of creaking branches reached them.

It was the sound of swiftness.

Elin leaned over him again, and this time, when she moved back it was to ready her bow. "It's going to climb the rock-face."

She was right. Large sections of the pattern were changing too rapidly, suggesting something fast. Its shape was only caught in glimpses, but it was long and seemed to possess many limbs… not at all round like a spider.

As if that matters.

"We don't have room to swing a weapon," Han was saying, his voice hard. "Draw knives. Keep it out."

Anyo did so, jaw clenched.

Croons continued as the menacing creature reached stone, colours rippling across its body when passing from tree to wall. It was like a chameleon – only far, far bigger and infinitely more deadly.

Trails of grey sludge followed its ascent, the exact source unclear.

Elin opened the fore window, stretched her bowstring and let a shaft fly.

The arrow thudded into the creature but did not slow it – the thing was now halfway to the carriage, still trailed by a line of grey… something. She closed the window with a frown.

"Let me," Nuvin said, lifting his two-pronged spear from where it rested opposite. "I will deter the creature from entering."

"While we do what?" Binya asked. "How are we supposed to stop it?"

"We try everything."

Anyo nodded.

The creature flung itself up the final few spans of mountain-face, now perched upon the gate. Its body remained difficult to discern from its surroundings, but it *was* long and lizard-like, with multiple legs and a weaving head bearing pale, milky eyes that did not blend.

And it waited.

Nuvin stood, weapon ready, everyone else gripping steel.

"I could move the carriage back, if it jumps," Katonga said. "Maybe there's a chance it would –"

Movement flashed.

Something heavy rocked the carriage. Anyo braced himself as above, the thing blocked some of the light. What limbs were visible seemed white, tinted green with standing hairs… yet those glimpses were interrupted by a wavering of the detail, almost like steam rising.

But heavy talons were clear.

The monstrous beast began to strike the windows – from

front and side, but despite the echoes each blow made, the heavy glass held. Strengthened somehow? A blessing, nevertheless.

Nuvin was chanting where he stood, and the sisters exchanged glances before Fiana spoke, without taking her eyes from the talons. "Where is the head?"

Anyo stared hard out his window, where no talons struck… and there, was that faint movement? But if it were the head, why weren't the eyes open? He glanced back to the other windows, and based on the shape of the thing, there was a chance… "It might be here."

Fiana tapped Nuvin on the shoulder and he nodded, still chanting.

"Change places, Anyo," Elin said, using her chin to gesture to her brother.

He did so with some difficulty in the crowded space. "What is he going to do?"

"Something he shouldn't. But if it works, we'll probably survive."

Now Nuvin lined his spear up with the window and, hopefully, the creature beyond – yet even with the extended reach, what was his plan?

The man was changing.

His skin was darkening… with fur! A rich brown, it grew from his hands and neck and face too, but that was not all. His shape began to change, shoulders and chest expanding, tearing but not destroying his clothing.

Even his eyes had grown larger, spaced wider to go with a dark nose. Like a bear? *How is this possible?* But it was, and a low growl now answered the crooning that had resumed from outside.

Nuvin tensed – and then thrust his spear.

The strengthened glass shattered.

The twin prongs hit something, penetrating deep enough to stick fast. The Sky Carriage rocked. It tore the spear from Nuvin's grasp but the creature was falling, ichor-covered body now visible.

And then it smashed through the trees below, vanishing.

Nuvin was breathing hard where he stood, body shrinking to his usual proportions and fur shedding, covering his torn clothing and soon, the steel floor too. He fell back and closed his eyes, still drawing deep breaths.

"Will he recover?" Anyo asked, and his relief was dampened by worry, similar concern on everyone's faces.

Elin was still on alert, arrow set to bowstring as Fiana knelt before her brother, lifting his eyelids. "Too early to say."

"What do you mean?"

She paused. "That he may not recover the ability to speak or even think like a man."

CHAPTER 9. – ANYO

"It is that serious?" Anyo asked.

Fiana took Nuvin's hands, glancing over her shoulder to answer. "*Aggisa-dah* is a cursed gift that only few can manage. It is not always possible for the link between person and animal to be denied when it has been invoked, and so it is rarely attempted."

"Do you mean, he would become a bear?" Binya asked.

She nodded. "First, a man reduced to instincts. In time, his body would change to a permanent mix of animal and person. It is a bitter thing to witness."

Elin had still not taken her gaze off the trees below. "He was able to shed, that's a good sign."

"It is," her sister agreed.

"There's something down below," Han said from the opposite window.

Anyo straightened. "Another creature?"

"No. It's man-made… I think it's a large handle resting against the rock face. Hard to see clearly."

"To open the gate?" Katonga asked.

"No way to know without climbing down."

"How?" Anyo asked. "We'd have to leave someone here with Nuvin; we can't have him alone."

"We will stay," Fiana replied. "Find a way through this place; we will protect him."

"Very well," he said. "So, how do we descend?"

Silence met his question. The distance was simply too far to drop, even with trees to break any fall. No-one carried rope, nor the means to fashion anything remotely similar. And the Sky Carriage quite obviously could not go down.

Which left the mountain, didn't it? *If such a surface can be scaled...*

Binya had seemingly come to the same conclusion, stretching out to push open the fore window. "The trail that thing left is stuck to the stone. Do you think we could use it?"

Anyo stepped over Fiana's legs to join Binya. It was a slim chance, surely? "We might have to try."

"We could end up stuck on the mountainside instead of being stuck in here," Katonga said. "There's always heading back to the clearing to take our chances with your brother."

Anyo hesitated. "That might be worse than this place. But I doubt we can rule it out."

"We need to be sure about the wall first, one way or another," Han said.

"We do." Once again with some difficulty, Anyo navigated through the Sky Carriage to the broken window, glass crunching underfoot. Elin gave him room and he used the palm of his hand to ram the remaining glass from the frame.

It fell into the trees below, but at some strain to his wrist.

Nevertheless, climbing free without cutting himself was now possible. He gripped the top of the carriage and exited slowly, so as not to rock the Sky Carriage… but considering its size and weight, he need not have worried. *Stable as the earth.*

Next, he reached for the grey substance and grimaced at its warmth. And texture. While he could get a firm grip, he could not tear it from the stone. Nor could he easily remove his hands. The creature's trail clung to his fingers and palms when he did. Both a heartening and troubling sign.

"Well?" Han called from within.

"It might actually take our weight. We could also become frozen in place upon the mountain." He shook his head. "It's too risky. I'll go alone."

"*That's* too risky, lad."

"Let me," Binya said.

He glanced back through the window frame to see a determined set to her jaw. "You must want to keep an eye on me."

She nodded, a smile almost gracing her lips. "I can't have you dying on me yet."

"I'll try first. If I get stuck, you'll all have to figure out a way to free me."

Anyo took a firm grip with his hands before stepping from the carriage and kicking into the sludge. But it was enough. Thankfully, the dome was not so steep, but as he wrenched one boot free and started down, pulling his hands out to find another handhold, there was enough of a change to his position that the sensation of falling backwards followed.

His stomach flipped. But he held steady long enough to adjust, even if his next step was harder to take. Anyo shouted up to Binya. "I think it's working, but you can't afford to stop."

"Right." Binya stood above him, reaching out for the wall herself.

Anyo continued down, focusing on the trail of gunk. While it was wide – another sign of the size of the creature – it was no singular, straight line. In places, it twisted and even split into multiple paths.

It was not enough to break his momentum, moving faster where the mountain was at least somewhat smooth, then taking some time to navigate protuberances or crevices. And while every placement of foot or hand became more difficult to free, each time he glanced down, the trees and then the loam-covered floor of the gorge grew closer until finally he was pulling himself free to stand upon firm ground with a sigh.

He spared only a glance for Binya, his coated hands too, before turning to seek the creature… and there, not too far away, in a heap of shattered branches and green and orange debris, lay the thing. Its skin was no longer able to match its surroundings; it was now a jumble of limbs, its huge body covered in green, patchy hair.

The head was not visible, but the monster hardly seemed alive – a sickly sweet stench already drifting through the wood.

"This is getting too hard, already," Binya said from directly above him, one foot kicking at the trail. "Returning could be a problem."

"One problem at a time." He stepped back. "You're close to the ground now."

Binya pulled herself free to drop down into a crouch. When she straightened, she did not spare the creature much time, instead focusing on her hands, which were just as coated as Anyo's. "We'd better try the lever, quickly."

Anyo glanced around and there, half-concealed by a shrub waited a cage of the same black steel with rigid patterns. And within, a heavy-looking handle.

They approached together, finding that the cage offered an opening large enough for one person to stretch a hand within.

Nothing indicated the purpose, but what else could it be?

He reached in to grip the lever and pull down, tensing up and even leaning back to add his weight to the task. But it clanked into position and the grinding of stone from high above followed. He grinned. "That sounded promising."

But the grin faded – opening his hand to release the handle was impossible.

He wrenched at it, a flash of pain running up his shoulder. "This is bad."

Cries of relief came from above, but he didn't answer yet.

"Wasn't this always going to happen?" Binya said as she wiped her own palms against the cage, with only mildly successful results based on what was left behind.

Anyo hung his head. "I suppose we found the limit to how long this stuff stays pliable, but we didn't have a choice. And you shouldn't help me, Binya. You'll only get stuck too."

"No. I will think of something." She flexed her fingers over and over as she paced the small clearing. "I doubt water will be enough. And based on the cage, we probably can't even cut your hand off."

Anyo looked up. "What?"

"Wouldn't that be better than being stuck here, waiting for another one of those things? Or other wild animals? Or death?"

"… Yes."

"Something wrong down there?" It was Katonga calling from the Sky Carriage.

Binya craned her neck. "Anyo is stuck."

Curses drifted down.

Her eyes widened, still looking up to the carriage, expression swiftly moving through surprise and even anger, before she kicked at the loam.

"What's wrong?"

"I almost don't want to say."

"You might as well; I'm not going anywhere any time soon."

She met his gaze. "I think I see a ladder up there. It's part of the Sky Carriage, connected to the underside."

He twisted, but the shrubs and trees made it hard to be sure. He groaned. "By Aehtu." If nothing else, it made sense that the designers of the Sky Carriage would include such a feature. *But why couldn't they have made it easy to recognise from inside?*

Binya lifted her voice. "Katonga, there's a ladder beneath the carriage."

His voice returned after a moment. "Are you certain?"

"Mostly. Is there some way to release it from inside?"

"We're looking."

One problem perhaps solved. He frowned down at the lever and his fingers, covered in the grey gunk and frozen in place. Even his free hand was hard to move, and he scraped it against the cage with less success than Binya.

"I do have an idea, while we wait," she said as she joined him.

"So long as it doesn't have sharp edges."

She smiled as she lifted a small pouch, opening it with some difficulty to reveal white sand. "Still dangerous."

"From the attack? I forgot you still had that."

"If I use it to rub my hands together, the friction might be enough."

"But everything Nuvin told us about the Moon Father..."

"I know. I don't have any other ideas." She knelt then, placing the pouch between her knees and doing her best to pull her hands free without destroying the bag. "The glow has completely left the sand, so that's enough for me."

"Wait," he said. "What if it isn't?"

"What if the only choice is to actually cut your hand off?"

"Wouldn't that be better than risking your life?"

"If you die from blood loss not long after, then no, it's not." She pulled one hand free at last, traces of cloth clinging, and grabbed a handful of the sand. Then she tore her other hand from the bag and rubbed both palms together.

Anyo held his breath.

She did not cry out or even shudder, was not overwhelmed by a silver-blue light nor did her body grow slack for her to stare up at the sky… she simply nodded to herself as she worked, flakes of grey falling away.

Within moments, her hands were mostly clear of the gunk and she chuckled. "I wasn't *absolutely* certain, you know."

He smiled. "I'm glad you took a chance."

"Your turn." She rose with the rest of the pouch, then reached in to pour some of the white grains across his skin, before setting to work rubbing and massaging. And while the monster's sludge flaked away from the outside easily enough, she had more trouble working the grains into creases between his skin and the steel.

But when his first finger was free, everything became a little easier.

With each subsequent success, he was able to put more pressure on freeing himself, allowing more grains sneak into the tiniest gaps and letting him rub against the handle until he was liberated. "Amazing, thank you."

And then Binya was pouring the last of the sand into his palm so that he could work on his other hand. It was a remarkable solution, and whether it was due to the sand itself or some lingering power from the glowing creature was not important for the moment.

Something rattled from above before he finished.

A ladder of steel rungs attached to what was a thinner but no less sturdy-looking set of wires hung just out of reach from a standing position, presumably having unfurled from the carriage above.

"Tell me that worked, right?" Katonga was calling.

"We're on our way," Anyo replied, and truly, having to jump up to reach the bottom rung was not such a problem compared to the narrow escape. He gestured to Binya. "Lead the way."

"Is this my reward for having saved you? To have to climb first?"

"Please accept my courtesy in place of anything better, until we're back home."

CHAPTER 10. – ROKURA

Being a prisoner was exceptionally dull.

Being a prisoner aboard a ship during a long sea-voyage was worse. The only company Rokura had been afforded was a single sailor, put in the brig for drunken scuffling. And that had been a mere night and a day, offering little in the way of conversation. After, it left only the cabin boy's deliveries of food and water to break up the time being chained to the bulkhead.

That, and two visits from Edazol.

The princess did not bother, which was no surprise. But Rokura's old master could not hide his disappointment when he did.

"There is no chance that you will be welcomed back to your old life now, but you can still act with honour when we land," Edazol had said, staring down at Rokura with arms folded. "Reveal the truth about the Senoja boy; where is he headed, what is his purpose, where will he use the relic to strike? Tell me at least that, and I will plead your case."

Rokura leant his head back against the hard wood with a sigh. "Iggy does not hail from Senoja, but Nokema. The rest of his story is not mine to tell."

"So you have claimed before."

"Yes."

Edazol stroked his moustache. "I never believed you were in the wrong, back in Anatoph, and I still do not, but I cannot fathom this hideous betrayal of your very nation – of everything you lived for. Did I not teach you better?"

"You taught me right and wrong, almost as much as my parents, Master."

"And?"

"And I would ask you, the Hearing – was it an excuse to strip me of my title, to avoid shame falling upon the king's name for my so-called betrayal?"

"It was an opportune moment, yes."

"I see."

"What of the boy?"

"I do not intend to place him in any more danger by sending Greyshields out to hunt him."

"Then you do know where he is heading?"

"I can guess."

"Will you force me to pry such information from you?"

"Yes."

The man threw his hands into the air. "Even if I were to believe your fanciful claim about his heritage, unlikely as it is, such a relic cannot simply be left in his hands."

"Clearly."

"Then do we in fact agree?"

"No," Rokura said. "But if you wanted to hold on to that box, you should have protected it better."

Edazol turned on his heel at that, and did not return for days – not until they were due to dock at Axoila. His former mentor wore a blade now, and was accompanied by two soldiers in their red cloaks, a pair of young Greyshields too – none whom Rokura recognised.

This time, Edazol came with no offers.

"We have reached the port city of Axoila in Viareya. You will accompany Her Highness on our hunt. You will follow her every order and in doing so, you may avoid execution for treason, but that is all. You are forever banished from Nasaru, and will not be returning when we leave these lands."

It was not precisely an empty threat, considering how difficult escape would be in the first place. And Edazol and the princess were not exaggerating when they mentioned execution.

The words could have made another wound, but after being cast out once, it hardly added much to the bitterness Rokura was already carrying. "Does Sorcerer Eroya's disc confirm that Brutan and the Duke have travelled here?"

"It does. We are pursuing them into the hills now." Edazol waved a hand to the soldiers. "Unchain and bring him to the princess."

"Yes, My Lord."

The men approached and freed Rokura without a word. One fellow handed Rokura his sword belt with its blades. Rokura glanced to Edazol.

"You are expected to pull your weight."

"I only stopped when you chained me here," he replied with a frown.

The tall man strode for the ladder, followed by his soldiers. Both Greyshields stayed behind and one, a man whose expression was placid – almost kind – gestured for Rokura to follow.

Rokura stretched his legs a moment then joined them.

The kind-faced man spun. His fist slammed into Rokura's side. Rokura fell to one knee, glaring up at the Greyshield. *I must be getting old – I didn't even see that coming, and I should have.* "And what is your name?"

"My name is Feboa, traitor." His face remained calm, but his hands were still clenched. "Know that I will be watching you."

The second lord, half his face hidden beneath a shadowy hood, reached out to pull Feboa back. "No need to keep Princess Kiteka waiting."

"Right." Feboa turned to follow Edazol.

Rokura rose with a grunt, walking after the second Greyshield, narrowing his eyes at the tenderness in his side. *I'm not getting old – I'm already there.*

Up on the decks, he entered a flurry of activity as sailors and soldiers alike worked to unload whatever goods were to be delivered; barrels and boxes in arm, crates being wheeled toward the gangway. Men were also readying the horses, all which seemed especially skittish. Would Arrow be safe back in Atanoph?

The wharf was filled with similar ships and squat beasts of burden at work on more goods. Shouts of workers carried across the water, while further along waited the city walls, pale stone climbing. Strangely, such walls stood with row upon row of narrow archer's slots in place – they created a uniform pattern and promised quite the hail of arrows.

Catapults were visible atop the battlements, like large, patient insects with their smaller fellows nearby; ballista mounted on regular platforms.

Axoila is signalling plenty of readiness to any who might attack.

Nearby, Princess Kiteka appeared to be thanking a Viareya official. The Axolian woman wore short pants and a leather jerkin – yet there was a formality about the armour, whose symbols seemed echoed on the steel rings upon her bare arms. She handed over a sealed scroll before striding back down the gangway.

The princess approached Rokura then, mouth tightening upon seeing him. She wore a breastplate and longsword at her waist. This time, her hair was fastened in braids. "Do you understand what you have been told?"

"I do."

"One ill-considered move and you are dead. Earn your life, if not your honour, by assisting in this rescue."

"I will."

"Show some gratitude," Feboa said with a grunt.

Rokura regarded the man a moment, then turned back to Kiteka. "Why has the Duke fled to Viareya? It makes little sense strategically, unless he has allies here?"

"That is what we mean to confirm."

She gave the order to disembark, and was soon enough leading everyone through the gates – courtesy of the sealed scroll, it seemed – and then into wide, paved streets beyond.

There, building materials were a mix of dark wood and bleached stone. Some of the rock was coloured, set in rows but used sparingly. Homes, it seemed, featured a pale orange while public buildings an equally muted green.

A striking design, but he did not have much time to admire it, since the princess kept their column moving quickly. She had them pass a large market where chiming music echoed, and more people in short items of clothing flocked, only allowing a stop for water and other supplies at the next gate, where a guide waited.

The guide was one Captain Ovedi, according to chatter Rokura overheard, not that he saw much of the man from the rear guard. And not that anyone would speak directly to 'the traitor' either, save for his tedious shadow, Feboa.

Without much in the way of delay, Captain Ovedi and his large force led them from the city along a stone highway and into an arid land. Yet it was not without beauty, Rokura soon saw. Stony hills surrounded them early in their journey, split into mysterious layers of colour. Compared to whatever was done to them in the city, outside, the stone was far more colourful. At the base, deep orange grew to white and then turned green, topped by a grainy yellow. Even the boulders and rubble strewn between the highway and the sheer hillsides were of similar shades, with faint spirals of pale dust rising.

Well. Hearing about the famous Coloured Coast was certainly nothing compared to seeing the place.

Along with rumours of its beauty were more concerning stories of certain passages of the hills that could mean blindness for those who travelled, or of raiders that would swoop down on strange, single wings to rob travellers, or of giant beasts that devoured the stone and anything else in its path... fanciful stories, perhaps.

The longer they rode, however, the more it seemed their black-leather-clad guides took time to warn the Princess and Edazol, gesturing often to the hills, light reflecting from their helms and bracers.

Or so it seemed from Rokura's position down the line. Essentially part of the rear guard, he was always surrounded by watchful eyes, be they soldier or Greyshield. And while the force of two score Nasaru was large enough to be quite noteworthy in a foreign land, the sight of eight Greyshields in one place was perhaps more. *Nine with me – not that I will lay claim to that name.*

But despite apparent concern from the captain and his soldiers, no attack came by nightfall. The large group had set up camp within a sparse field, not too distant from a small, unnamed town. Its walls were built of the same coloured stone as the surrounds, making it quite difficult to spot from a distance. But the silvery, pale trunks of the native trees and their thin flowers, appearing more like tresses of hair, did break up the colour.

The field stood ringed by the same trees, joined also by shrubs somewhat closer to green, their scent close to… mint? Or it might have been something more peppery; at least, it seemed as much when Rokura found himself searching through them for firewood.

"Can't believe they won't let us inside – I was looking forward to a real bed after that bloody ship," one of the soldiers was saying to another.

"Me too. But I'm not surprised."

"You're not?"

"You've never been to Viareya, right?" the second man asked.

"First time."

"Well, even if they have an inn large enough, it's not part of our permission, apparently. Not until the bigger places – if we have to travel that far, I guess. This is the first time I've left the port city."

"Think we'll go that deep? I hear that Tuaxo has amazing gardens."

The first soldier chuckled. "I've heard *other* stories, to be honest."

"You do think about things other than women, don't you?" the second asked with a sigh.

"Sometimes, I do."

Rokura wiped sweat from his brow and continued his search. Unlike the seemingly well-travelled soldier, his own knowledge of Viareya was not first-hand. He was aware, at the least, that everyone's movements were monitored and apparently controlled closely. Especially if they wanted to enjoy assistance from local forces.

Captain Ovedi would likely have such orders, in any event. Which raised the question, were Brutan and the Duke being helped by someone in Viareya? *If so, why here?* Bedoa had plenty of trade connections but helping Takirov rebels smuggle Nasaru children across the sea to a foreign land was precisely the sort of act that could stir an invasion… should the king be willing to admit to Asaro's existence, of course.

And if that was actually the man's purpose… madness.

What exactly did the princess know?

Sure as I am holding back information, she's playing the same game.

He glanced back toward where she and Edazol stood together, their words inaudible – and suddenly, it was all too easy to suspect some bizarre treachery. He snorted at his own doubts. *The answer is far simpler. They simply do not trust you now.*

For 'Lord' Rokura, Greyshield, once trusted and relied upon by his king, was a Lord no more.

Now, merely Rokura – widower and Exile.

CHAPTER 11. – ROKURA

The highway turned down between striped hills, disappearing into a shadowy ravine whose walls were lined with alcoves, old rockslides and uneven trails that suggested perfect vantages for ambush.

And of course, the old road they travelled was all the more suitable, considering it offered the only option leading to the sheer, windswept cliffs where Brutan and the Duke were suspected to lurk.

At least according to Captain Ovedi.

Rokura glanced from the coloured ridges and occasional rows of silvery shrubs, then back to the local soldiers. Their bows, hammers and maces were all held ready and helms were moving often. They *did* appear quite vigilant, but no word was passed from the vanguard for any additional level of watchfulness.

Had the scouts returned yet?

It's all a little imprudent. Especially when information about the Duke's passage had been shared so freely by the guards in the town they'd already passed. Such tangible proof of the Duke's treachery drove the princess and Edazol to quicken the column's pace, but the cost was caution.

Yet when Rokura requested that one of his minders send a message against rushing after the Duke, the man returned from the vanguard with no response. Of course Her Highness might well offer the disdain of silence to the messenger, but surely the warning itself was sound.

The other Greyshields were not quite so watchful as the Viareya, but despite their relative youth, they knew their roles well, hands never too far from their weapons, gaze roving the unfamiliar landscape or watching the princess.

But the farther their force moved into the ravine, the darker it became, the more unsettled their guides grew. Several times he noted them dismounting to examine the earth and later, when the column had stopped to water the horses and take a moment's rest, Rokura started toward Princess Kiteka.

She and Edazol were speaking with Captain Ovedi, his expression one of concern. He was a short fellow, but stocky – full of muscle, and he wore no helm. Instead, his bald head was painted white, its significance unclear.

A hand fell on Rokura's shoulder. "Your position is right here."

Feboa, his face almost corpse-like in its calm.

Rokura frowned. "Something is amiss. I am going to learn what has Captain Ovedi concerned."

"You'll learn when you are told."

"Is that so, lad?"

The Greyshield nodded again, his expression not changing. "You're not important – you'll have to grow accustomed to that, traitor. And while you do, I won't be accepting anything that makes my life harder."

"If that is true, you should be more concerned."

"You choose to threaten me from a poor position."

Other men had moved closer, none close to drawing blades, but all expectant.

Rokura sighed. "You really are young. Tell me, where are our scouts? What are the Sorcerers doing to look ahead? Why are our guides so watchful? Why were they examining the ground where I see only dust and stone? Why does Captain Ovedi speak to Her Highness with concern upon his face? These are extremely basic questions."

Feboa was shaking his head.

"Traitor or no, he is right," one of the soldiers said as he stroked his beard. "Something is obviously afoot."

Rokura waited. Feboa had not stood aside. Yet the younger man's next action or whatever words he might have meant to share, whatever it might have been, was interrupted by a tall figure striding into the circle.

Edazol was frowning, his grey moustache in some disarray. A sign of concern, perhaps.

"Assemble. Her Highness and Captain Ovedi will address you."

Men and women followed the Master to where the groups had fallen into ranks, Greyshields up front beside the Viareya infantry and to the rear… *Me and my minder.*

But Princess Kiteka was easy to hear. "Captain Ovedi has troubling news. He expects an attack by the time we reach the cliffs." Her expression was hard. "As we are visitors here, I will defer to his wisdom – and let me add, it is already too late for us to seek another path. The Stone Mammoth will prevent us from our goal; we will have to face it in some form."

Not a single murmur passed through the men, but several

exchanged glances. A tiny break in discipline, but it hardly mattered, all things considered.

Nor is it my place to remind them. Lord no more. Instructor no more.

The Viareya soldier stepped up beside the princess. "In your language, I am not a wordsmith. I will be brief. The Stone Mammoth is difficult to describe. An enormous beast. They are rare. They roam the hills and plains, seeking… a special stone. The specific word in your tongue escapes me but all who stand in its way are crushed." He gestured to the picketed horses. "The young are two or three times bigger than a horse. Adults five times as large. Their hide is thick – aim for the eyes. Strike from afar. The underside is softer, but that is all. They are not fast, but you would be lucky to survive just one blow from their paws."

Silence met his words until Edazol stepped from the line of soldiers to address everyone. "I trust no-one doubts our hosts here. I have seen a babe, in previous travels. It was exactly as described. Our scouts have witnessed one approaching the cliffs; it has caught the scent of the minerals it craves within and it will shatter the stone walls. If we do not intervene, our quest has been for naught."

"How can we defeat something like that?" one of the soldiers asked.

Ovedi lifted his heavy axe. "With these, if the Lords of the Earth are willing. But first, we will let your targets defend against the Mammoth. Then, we defeat the survivors. Your sorcerers will sharpen your weapons to better penetrate the hide. But even if you agree to my plan, I cannot guarantee all will survive."

Edazol raised a hand at the swelling of questions. "There is no other choice. We will not be defying the orders of Her Highness, let alone our king. Survival is never guaranteed, as all here know. You may, if you choose, turn in your cloaks and forfeit your titles, the rest of you, your rather generous pay."

Rokura almost smiled at the lack of participants in such a gesture. But he did raise his voice. "Our reasons are clear, Edazol. What will Captain Ovedi and his men risk their lives for?"

Princess Kiteka straightened. "That question is beneath even you, former Lord Rokura."

Even me, huh? "We are lucky to have their assistance, yes, but it is a simple question and one that I would ask of any ally."

Captain Ovedi raised a hand to forestall what could have become an argument, considering the princess' expression. "Our alliance is important – but you are correct. There is another reason. The death of a Stone Mammoth is worth a fortune to any man. Even if he was only a scavenger. We will all take this risk to provide for our families for years."

Rokura raised an eyebrow. An honest, if unexpected answer. "And such fortune is even to be shared amongst all those here?"

Now Edazol pointed with a snarl. "Still your tongue, Rokura!"

Rokura stared back at his one-time master. The man might have been correct, in the end. There really was no need to antagonise… not while the risks were so great. *Oyo would have scolded me. I can almost hear her voice as it is.*

Nevertheless, a small, petty part of him could not deny some pleasure in the exchange.

But Captain Ovedi had not seemed to take any offence. "None will miss out. But once more, this is not a 'stag hunt', as I believe the term is in Nasaru."

Princess Kiteka cast her gaze across those gathered. "We must reach the Duke's lair before dawn breaks. Go now and rest and prepare – and see the sorcerers before we leave." She waved a hand before turning for her mount, motioning for Edazol to follow.

Captain Ovedi and his men remained to further discuss tactics against the Stone Mammoth, and while plenty stayed to listen, just as many of the soldiers and Greyshields were already making a queue before the sorcerers. They had spread out in a small half circle and were discussing how best to use their supply of Black Coral.

Rokura joined neither group, instead turning his attention back to the layered hills and their silvery trees.

One problem had not been addressed. Exactly how many soldiers – Takirov, Nasaru, local or otherwise – were waiting inside the cliffs with Brutan and the Duke?

CHAPTER 12. – MEI

The Guardian climbed four storeys and spread across land that would have contained three of the surrounding buildings, most of which were merchants, with the one right next door selling flowers.

And it seemed the innkeeper was a regular customer of the flower shop, for trellises covered the stone in not only a functional manner, but also decorative one, with strips of flowers woven within. Some of the bare stone boasted enclaves with dark pots containing fruit trees, and even the landing platform upon the roof, where a rope basket was arriving, stood flanked by small trees, their rings of white and yellow flowers bright.

"There is another way," Thorn said as he turned from the main entry and its open doors, the pleasant din of the midday meal drifting out. She even caught a glimpse of a serving boy delivering steaming rice and vegetables. Her stomach rumbled.

Another servant approached, the heavyset man offering to take their horses with a deferential nod, to which Thorn agreed.

Next, he started down the nearest side street, stepping aside to allow a mother carrying her babe to pass, before taking a key from his clothing. He used it to unlock a bolted door with a vaguely familiar word painted upon it, then admitted them into a darkened passage.

Next came a set of stairs – a beautiful wooden spiral. He led her to the top floor where a wider corridor waited, this one lined by windows. Thin fabric cut into patterns had been overlain on the glass, allowing a golden light to replicate the shapes upon pale timber walls.

Far more decorative than home, but it doesn't seem out of place either. Like something we might have once done ourselves.

Yet another servant dressed in a dark costume approached, arms laden with bedding, and she paused to bow to Thorn. "Welcome home."

"Thank you, Helavi. I hope you are well."

"I am."

She continued down the passage but Thorn stopped before a door with a large number carved into the surface – not unlike that used for 'seven' in Nokema. How many more similarities would she find? *They might not matter in the end, but there's no way to avoid noticing.*

Mei looked back to Thorn, who was already halfway into the room, words from the servant sinking into her awareness a little after the fact. "They know you here?"

He paused. "Of course. This is my inn; they all know me."

"Just how long have you been staying here, then?"

"When I say my inn, I mean the inn that I own."

She stared after him a moment before following. *Exactly who is this man?* What had he been doing since he left Nokema, to now own such a large inn? It *did* explain how everyone had treated him. Also his key.

The room featured a regular bed, but also a hammock strung across one corner, just as stories described upon a ship, but why? The place also featured a strange… pit in the centre of the room, this lined with cushions. Was it for sitting on?

The same coloured windows here bore a thin screen, perhaps to slide across? So it seemed, since there was a lever, which Thorn used to change the light's colour to something cooler. For a moment, twin colours had fallen upon a big, porcelain bath with clawed feet.

That looks tempting.

Thorn gestured to the lever. "As you can see, this lets you select a colour for the light, if you wish, but the rest of the place is like any other room you might come across in any other inn, for the most part."

He started back across the polished boards.

"I have more questions."

"Call for Helavi and she will run a bath or bring a meal. She knows how to make wonderful pajen-bread if you didn't want to try Senoja cuisine. I will be in my room below; rest until I return."

"No," Mei said with a frown. "I meant about your plans."

Thorn stopped at the door. "And you shall have your chance. You must be patient."

"A fine thing to say to your prisoner."

"Helavi will return with your key soon," he replied as he closed the door behind him.

Mei muttered a curse beneath her breath before turning back to the room where she moved to the window. There, she tapped her foot as she stared down at the street, where a stream of Senoja in their colourful coats and tunics slid by.

Just how much of what Thorn said was true? He wasn't trustworthy. He harboured his own goals regarding the mysterious Moon Father. His power outweighed hers, and if he wanted Iggy, he was an enemy.

Was there a way to use Thorn to reach Iggy? "After all, he wants to use us," she muttered.

If only I could speak to Arun. Or warn Iggy.

Mei exhaled as she returned to the door, opened it and poked her head out. "Helavi?"

The woman soon appeared from another room with a welcoming smile. "Yes, dear?"

"Thorn told me that I should ask you if I wanted anything." Thanks to the earring, Mei had understood Helavi. She spoke Inora herself, and it was either close enough that the Senoja woman followed, or all the time spent weaving thoughts and voice together while travelling with Mamalo was helping. *Has he really recovered? Is he following me?* It might have been safer if he didn't.

"By the look of all that dust and grime on your face, I'm guessing: bath and meal?"

Mei raised a hand to her cheek. "Y-yes, please."

"Don't worry, I'll organise everything," she said as she produced a key of brass, the number seven engraved upon the bow. "You just go inside and rest a short while."

"Thank you."

Mei returned and slumped across the bed but did not have to wait long for Helavi to appear, delivering a meal of butter spread across toasted bread and sweet fruits before filling the bath and leaving with a smile.

The meal was delicious – Mei nearly inhaled the whole lot,

but managed not to choke, at least. Once her hunger had been sated, she moved to the bath and undressed, dipping a toe into the water before climbing in. Heat enveloped her body, muscles relaxing, tension vanishing – or at least, receding.

Even as a captive, taking a chance to rest for but a brief time was still worthwhile. She started by running the washcloth across her forearms, an old cut appearing from beneath the dirt. "Hmmm." *I can't even remember where that came from.* How long searching now? And why was it only after being forced to stay in Senoja that she'd finally come close to reaching Iggy?

Possibly, at least. *You have to admit, you want to believe Thorn about how close Iggy is.*

Depending on exactly what the suspicious Exile had in mind, Mei would be a fool not to take her chance to both call Iggy *and* warn her brother. That way, when he arrived, he'd be ready. *Together, we might have a chance of escaping.* Mei lay her head back against the porcelain, the hot water touching the ends of her hair.

There was another possibility, of course – protect Iggy, as she ought to.

Instead, I have to tell him to stay away from this place.

She slid deeper into the water, letting it reach her chin now. "Escaping is my problem."

***

Thorn himself had bathed and eaten and changed into armour, now wearing one of the pale breastplates she'd only half-noticed on the gate guards. And while his face was not clean-shaven, generally speaking, he did seem at least a little neater. "I will answer your questions. Come with me to the Sealed

Garden."

"I have one before we leave," she said.

"Yes?"

"Who are you, here in Senoja? You wear local armour and own an enormous inn and you are about to take me, another foreigner, to what is supposedly one of the most dangerous places in this land. Who are you?"

He smiled. "Something akin to a Paragon."

"Even as an outsider?"

"Yes. Now, we have a carriage waiting downstairs."

Once again, he led her through the quieter parts of the inn and then out into the side-street where a carriage and two white horses waited. The carriage was not so tall as those in Nasaru, sleeker in design, but perhaps unsurprising for Kaarsi, the use of rope was prominent. Not just the tri-coloured thread in the hitching ropes or the pattern echoed in the leather reins, but also lining the inside of the wheels themselves. Decorative, only – but once again, why was the whole place so fixated on rope?

A swishing sound ran overhead, as if in answer, as another basket swung down toward the river.

"Still curious? It is quite fun when you're young, at least," Thorn said as he pulled open the carriage door.

She stepped inside without responding.

Thorn sat opposite, staring out the window as the team of horses drew them forward. As the ride continued, passing more buildings with their round windows and coloured glass, it seemed he would remain silent.

"Where is this Sealed Garden?"

"On the outskirts of the city, accessible only during low-tide.

A quiet place that few care to visit, either way. They consider it haunted." He spoke without turning, and in one hand he seemed to be polishing a small stone of milky white… yet the colour also boasted a brilliant, rainbow-like pearlescence.

"And instead of discussing your goals, and how you will achieve them, we are going to sit in silence?"

"It is easier to show you."

Mel leant forward a little. "Then tell me about how you expect I can lure Iggy here – where is he now?"

"Some days away. After this little visit, we'll return to the inn where you will eat and rest – for we rise before dawn. We can send your call at sunrise."

"Then, I'm just calling to him with my mind?" She had tried as much in the marsh, and achieved nothing. Obviously, Thorn had some better idea.

"I will lend you my strength. On top of which, we will be standing within the Wild Shell of Evorsi."

Each answer only offered more questions. "Is this wild shell also located within the Sealed Garden?"

"No."

"Then, where is it?"

He placed the stone into a pocket and crossed his legs at the ankle. "Lady Filjanes."

"Then you know her, due to your status here in Kaarsi?"

"No – we will be using the Shell without permission," he replied "But you need not worry. I have already made the necessary arrangements."

CHAPTER 13. – MEI

Low tide revealed what Thorn had brought her to see. Within a gently sloping cove, sheltered by a stone archway that towered over them, the rock garden waited in sand. Scattered with puddles and rivulets, the seawater was turning orange beneath a setting sun.

"Our timing is excellent," Thorn had said as he'd led her closer.

Crossing the beach had taken some courage, considering the Luminous Children, as Thorn was now calling them, and even the roaring of the vast ocean seemed ominous. Unnerving, even, considering its size. But once she slid down the wet sand and her boots hit smooth stone, her concern receded.

It really was a garden, in its own way.

A mix of uneven stone and faded coral, some sections melted smooth and others quite coarse and jagged, stretched before her. The high-water mark suggested the surface would usually be hidden at some depth. So, too, the tide would have concealed small stumps and rows of cloven stone that protruded, as though seats, benches and fence-posts or walls had once stood.

In its centre, Thorn stood over a glittering bank of pearls. They had been arranged into that of a face – a young woman with a look of determination.

"I can't believe people haven't stolen these," Mei said.

"If you place a hand upon her face, you will see what she has sealed away, and why no-one dares offer her even that shred of comfort; human touch." His explanation was… unexpected, along with the trace of sadness in his tone.

"And that will be the proof you mentioned?" Mei asked as she crouched before the pearls.

"You do not need it, but yes. The Moon Father is seeking freedom from the twin seals, and you will witness his spectre. Steel yourself if what you have seen up to now is lacking, and you still mean to do this, Mei."

She met his gaze.

"And know that I will help you."

"… You will help?"

"The aftermath is not pleasant."

Mei hesitated, then put both hands on her hips. No more delays. Even if he was right and she *had* seen plenty to be concerned about, this moment could not be ignored. *Don't I have to witness it for myself?*

She knelt to press her palm against the pearls.

A web of burning stars in blue and white replaced the beach, the shadows seeming to *simmer* where they lurked between drifting threads of luminosity.

But there was no heat, no cold against her skin either.

No sense of menace…

She rose. Where was the so-called Moon Father?

From beyond the stars, a murmuring reached her. Inora words – but soft, from a deep voice who urged her closer. And she took a step toward it before planting her feet more firmly. "No." Her voice did not echo. The word came out softer than she'd intended, as if something in the air had suppressed sound.

Before her, a face was pushing up through the sand. Far larger than human, its uncertain features were widespread, almost turtle-like; covered in wrinkles, eyes bright. The mouth dropped open, grains trailing, and still only silence.

But a desire was clear as the purest crystal.

To come forth and devour, to send a tide of luminous sand to replace every living creature until only enough remained to be raised, like cattle –

That should be enough.

The voice cut through, and the beach and its fading light and sunset-rivulets returned, a warm hand upon her shoulder too – Thorn.

She glanced up at him as a trembling started, heart racing. Some of the heartbeats were too hard, and irregular. Every skipped beat caused her whole body to clench, waiting for it to restart. "I…" Once again, her heart stopped, just long enough to have panic dry her mouth, to shrink the cove around her to a single point while she waited for another heartbeat. Terror mounted.

His wrinkled face returned – the Moon Father was inside her mind!

"No." Mei squeezed her eyes shut.

By the Guardians, he's going to use me *as a path to freedom, he's going to escape through me, he's going to steal my voice, he's going to burn my organs blue, he's going to wring me out like a wet rag –*

Thorn squeezed her shoulder. *No, he's not. Listen to me, Mei. That is his echo. You are safe. He cannot reach you – I will banish what lingers.*

And then soft, sweet, empty darkness.

But she did not lose consciousness. Instead, she opened her

eyes to the rock garden and the whispers of a calm ocean once more. The waves were creeping closer, but Thorn had already pulled her to her feet.

Gratitude rushed through Mei and she held his hand perhaps a moment longer than she'd needed to get her balance. Her panic was still dissolving; breathing even enough, but had a single grain of the Moon Father remained behind, something buried within the deepest parts of her mind?

No, I'm free.

And it was clear why people avoided the place.

"Help me, Mei. Let's call your brother and together we will destroy Kaziuu, the Moon Father, before he breaks free."

She drew in a shuddering breath. "How much time is there?"

"We have time, if we can draw Iggy here." Thorn pointed to the arrangement of pearl, to a corner where many actually appeared dull, several had even turned black. "When the rest of the pearls go dark, we will know that we are too late."

She nodded. "Before, you said something about twin seals. The other seal is within the Moon Gate, right?"

"Yes. But when I reached it, the pearls were already darkened."

Mei straightened. "What about the village?"

"They are in no more danger than the rest of us."

"You said they've forgotten."

"The Paragons will sense the Grains for what they are – you did, even without the knowledge that has been lost. Or perhaps, knowledge that had been kept from you. They will flee if they must, but the Moon Father's attention is on this seal, for *this* is what he must break to free himself." He started back toward the beach. "And this is where I will cast him down."

CHAPTER 14. – MEI

Mei was already pacing her room in the gloomy predawn, trying with limited success to banish the wide, wrinkled face of the Moon Father from her memory, when Thorn knocked upon the door.

It was all too easy to believe nothing had changed.

She was still a prisoner and Thorn's methods still painted him as untrustworthy. She was still planning to escape, somehow, and she would be *warning* Iggy, rather than simply calling him. Beyond that… well, locating Iggy would be enough at first.

But now, she and Iggy would have to find a way to deal with Kaziuu and his children.

It was a threat that could not be ignored.

Afterwards? Afterwards was far more uncertain. Together they could… what, exactly? *Find a new place to call home.* Mei sighed as she lifted both hands to rub at her temples. Wasn't that simply more wishful thinking? Dangerous, foolish thinking, in fact. Especially when it came to the Moon Father. *Just how strong do you think you are? Even with Iggy, you won't be enough.*

Her limits were as obvious as they'd always been – defeating one Grain had cost too much, how could she possibly hope to face down an army of them? Each step in her restless pacing became a little harder until she was almost stomping. *We'd need Thorn's power too.* More. *Guardians be damned!*

And so her thoughts had circled between surety and doubt, all through a fitful sleep the night before, and all through her pacing across the smooth boards beneath her feet now, to the moment that Thorn knocked.

"Mei."

She crossed the room and opened the door to find her captor, now dressed all in black with a hook and rope strapped at his waist. "What else do you have up your sleeve, Thorn? Because you, me and Iggy won't be enough."

A flicker of surprise passed over his face. "It is heartening to realise that you are now more willing to –"

"I won't call my brother here just so that we can all die together."

"That is not my plan."

"Then share it!" she snapped. Thorn started down the corridor, this time heading for the common room, it seemed. "There is something we can use to bolster our strength, but we need your brother to attain it to begin with."

"*You* need him," she said as she followed with a frown, passing a pair of young customers who gave them looks of concern.

Thorn's explanation had been a tiny bit better than what he usually offered but was still unsatisfactory.

Once outside and once more within a carriage, wheels rumbling over stone, he spoke again. Yet not exactly what she expected. "What do you know of the *Kel-ani*, the so-called Sun-Killers?"

"Not a lot." *Which is strange, especially after being accused of being one.* "The stories I heard usually mentioned their ability to go unseen, to kill even in bright sunlight."

"The ability is more a power they exert over those around them. They can convince a person's mind to see a lie, to see only an absence. That is where they strike; they are not truly able to become invisible. It is something Nokema has forgotten, but in exchange, we tend to be stronger in terms of brute force."

He was obviously warning her for a reason. "Will this noblewoman have Sun-Killers?"

"Several. And I will need you to help me deal with them."

"Very well," she said, and though her tone was calm enough, just how difficult would it be?

"Good. Seek them with your mind; it will be easy. If in doubt, I imagine someone of your strength will actually 'hear' or 'see' before they strike."

"What does that mean?"

"It's different for everyone, but you'll know when it happens."

The carriage began to slow. *Looks like I'm going to find out before too long.*

Thorn bade the driver wait, striding toward the looming shadows of a mansion – several storeys tall, its windows dark and no sign of any rope baskets upon its roof.

But light at a steel gate revealed a pair of soldiers. Like the guards at the city walls, the two wore white breastplates and winged helms. Unlike Thorn, these men also wore gauze over their breastplates, a blue almost black in the growing light, and all-in-all, a little impractical.

Both soldiers moved forward to meet them with unwelcoming expressions. "Return after dawn if you have business here," the taller one said.

Mei barely glanced at him as Thorn's calm explanations receded into the background. Instead, she used her mind to search the gardens; green leaves shaped as little hearts peeking between steel bars. The tops were sharpened into points like spearheads, just as unwelcoming as the guards.

Despite Thorn's warning, there seemed to be no-one else guarding the mansion – no sense of any of the Sun-Killers.

A silvery bell rang within her mind.

From behind!

Mei spun and there, a long dagger wavered in the air, almost transparent as it approached, held by unseen hands. Sun-Killer! Mei lashed out with her mind and something heavy hit the stones, blade clattering away.

A figure clothed in white and grey, close-fitting garb with a veil and another blade belted at her waist, appeared on the ground. Motionless, but breathing, at least.

"Well done," Thorn said.

Mei glanced back to the guards. Both were returning to their post, moving as though nothing at all had happened mere paces from where they stood. More, they continued on to the gates and actually opened them. "What did you do?"

"They see what I want them to see which, right now, is their master coming home. Now hurry," he added.

She leapt after, barely keeping up as he ran between the gates.

A paved courtyard waited beyond, half-filled with wagons. Most were covered, but not enough to conceal all of what was inside, which seemed to be silks and small boxes and vials marked by symbols that did not look like either Senoja or Nasaru markings. No guards patrolled within, but there were three doorways to choose from – each bearing a bright lamp.

Thorn turned immediately to the left, opened the door and led her back out onto the moon-lit grounds and toward a stable. There, horses slept, their bodies strangely upright. But he did not go to them for some part of his plan, to create a diversion, perhaps, but instead moved around to the side where bales of hay were stacked.

When he started to climb them, she glanced up to where the roof met part of the mansion walls… and there, vines grew up a lattice of rope. *Oh.*

Mei dug her hands into the hay and climbed after.

"Are you still watching for more Sun-Killers?" Thorn asked.

She hadn't stopped precisely… "Aren't you doing that too?"

"No. I'm doing everything else. And there's one in the tree off to your left – he's tying a string to his bow right now."

Mei twisted and there again, a glimpse of pale movement – a translucent bow being bent by invisible hands. Why were only the weapons visible? No time to ask Thorn. She flung a blast of power across the distance; a harder blow than before, to make sure it still stunned the Sun-Killer.

The sound of crashing branches followed, and then a thump. *I guess that was enough.*

"Right through their defences – impressive," Thorn said as he extended a hand and helped her up onto the roof.

"What do you mean?" she asked once she'd found her footing upon the boards.

"As I've said before, like many from Nokema, you're stronger than most," he replied, impatience in his voice. "Now, to the ropes."

Mei reached between the vines to grip the lattice, following

Thorn as quickly as she could.

"Isn't this inviting an attack? Or at least thieves?" Mei whispered as she passed a darkened window.

"The vanity of such decoration aside, there are other forms of guards and alerts in place, but as I said, I'm dealing with that."

And the sense of his power became more obvious, as if he'd allowed her a glimpse of what he was doing. How it spread across the mansion, how it was at work in many places at once, dealing with things she did not understand, but knew at least were connected to their gift.

Finally, Mei reached the top – a sparse roof-garden. It featured only a row of potted plants and a large dais of sand, which could be accessed via two stone steps. In the centre of the sand waited the huge form of Evorsi's Wild Shell, whatever that meant.

The growing light revealed a patterned surface – tiger stripes in pink, red and white… most unlike the shells she'd seen in the rivers near home. It was long and cone-shaped, tapering off toward one end, with the other a pale, smooth opening.

"What is it doing up here, in the middle of the roof?"

Thorn shrugged. "What happens to all precious things when the obscenely wealthy find them – nothing. It is merely held captive here, for but a few to gaze upon."

"And what about me?"

"Stand upon the Shell and call to your brother. It will send your words across the land on swift wings; he will hear you. I will help, also."

She nodded slowly. "And what about everyone else with telekinesis? Won't anyone with our gifts be able to hear me, if this is going to be so powerful? And how will Iggy find us – he doesn't know Kaarsi."

"Usually you might be overheard, yes."

"But?"

He sighed. "But I will cloud the location of your call, of course. We will have enough time to flee. Don't worry, he will be able to find us because he can find *you*."

"I see." But she didn't fully. The details were not necessarily so important – not compared to nearly being able to speak to Iggy at last, after so long. Mei approached the Shell and reached out to rest one hand upon its cool, exceptionally smooth surface. Her pulse quickened and she took a deep breath. *Finally*.

"Are you ready, then?"

"I am."

CHAPTER 15. – ANYO

Anyo stared down at the Senoja village and its painted rooftops with a grin, dawn light very soft where it tinted chimney smoke. It wasn't easy to control his features, to push back with prudence against the hope that churned in his chest. *There's a real chance we've actually found a proper clue this time.*

"Calm down," Binya said from beside him, a smile on her own face. "Nuvin himself said he might be wrong."

"At least he can speak to tell us, now," he replied. And it had been a long time *after* their successful crossing upon the Sky Carriage, and passage from the mountain and down into Senoja lands before he seemed himself. At first, Nuvin could not walk unaided, and after that, while he understood whatever was said to him, the man had not been able to speak until leaving the mountains. "But I can feel it." Anyo made a fist. "We're closing in on Misha's trail."

The Lirayx glanced back to the camp, a relatively uncluttered space barely visible between the stone pillars and ruined buildings. "Sometimes you've got a boyish excitement, you know."

That sounds better than being called 'obsessed', at least. "I do?"

"You do. Just try not to let that fact make the inevitable fall even harder if we don't find anything here," she replied. "This is the fourth village, you know."

"And three before this group," he said with a nod. Yet it hadn't dampened his spirits at all, since each time there had been a little information gleaned, either from the animals or the people. Still no grave, but if the village of Rsiani below turned out to have nothing much, well, they *were* nearing the Singing City of Liialle.

Even so, at nearly each stop there had been stories of foreign singers – plenty of them. The trouble had been determining which tales might have related to Rinbe's wife, since many were plausible.

Save for the story of an especially talented singer passing through, notable due to her status as a foreigner who could perform flawlessly in Senoja.

Standing against such gains was a problem anticipated but still difficult to solve. The farther west they travelled, the more the group stood out amongst the villages they visited. It made gathering information a little harder, with looks of suspicion or outright hostility becoming common.

So far, only once had violence arisen – courtesy of soldiers in their bone-white breastplates and coloured gauze, but there had been no deaths, at least.

Would the village of Rsiani be any different in that respect?

It appeared much like the others; rectangular homes half-sunk into the earth, with upper storeys usually containing only one room, giving the buildings a somewhat pointed shape. The tiles were painted in colourful patterns, a tradition said to come from their ancestors' desire to communicate with the gods.

Actually seeing such bright decoration was far more interesting than reading about it at his tutor's knee.

"I have been meaning to congratulate you, you know," Binya said as she moved a little closer. "You don't seem so consumed by our pact, anymore."

He nodded slowly. "With everything that's happened since, meeting Nuvin and the sisters, the Sky Carriages and… that thing, and being trapped… and now the progress we're making… well, there hasn't been time to worry."

"Then you've accepted things as they are?"

"I'm not sure I'd go that far," he said with a small frown. "I just can't waste any time to focus on that now. But I do have one request, actually."

"Oh?"

"Without telling me, I want you to give me a warning if it looks like I am going to betray myself."

She raised an eyebrow. Up close, the smoothness of her skin was quite pleasing. "Can you be a little more specific?"

"If you see me make a decision that goes against what you know I truly believe, warn me. Especially if it is something I have yet to realise about myself."

Binya exhaled, as if in doubt, but she only nodded and did it seem… was she impressed? Or just surprised?

"Is that a promise?" he asked her.

"More like agreement. Agreement to a request from the one who has hired me." Once more, it was difficult to tell what she was thinking.

"Good enough."

A hiss cut through the quiet that followed. Anyo spun to find Fiana waving for them to follow. "Soldiers – they've surrounded us."

"What?"

"Han suggested we three run. At least, I think that's what he meant," she said, but the young woman's expression made it clear she did not want to do so.

"How many?" Anyo asked.

"I saw half a dozen, but there could be more."

Anyo glared back to the ruins, but the stones revealed nothing, of course. Abandoning the others was out of the question. And there was a chance the Senoja would not be truly hostile... or was that simply wishful thinking?

"We're probably running out of time," Binya said.

Anyo nodded and set off for their camp, reaching and then weaving through the place, keeping crumbling stone between his position and the faint flicker of firelight.

There, over a dozen soldiers waited. They wore much the same clothing and armour as those who accompanied various dignitaries to the palace back home – a pale mesh that appeared as chainmail, or breastplates of a similar material, with coloured gauze worn over the top. The gauze was not only ornamental but spoke of the Path such men and women had chosen. Here, the dozen soldiers wore a mix of yellow and red, with two green glimpses also.

Hard to recall what it all means, but yellow and red tended to suggest they mostly consider themselves vengeful protectors and the green was for warrior-healers...

All carried short bows and narrow-bladed short swords, most with hands upon their hilts or bows held ready, if not drawn.

"We will try diplomacy," Anyo said softly.

"Are you certain?" Binya asked.

He nodded. "Anything else will only hinder our chances of searching. And our lives."

Anyo hailed the campsite, approaching with arms raised. The circle of soldiers admitted him, and a slender fellow wearing a silver circlet approached, no doubt their leader, the Sivelii. He had the typical Senoja pale skin and blue eyes, and a long scar running from his jaw down toward his breastplate. It was not an old scar either, since it was still held together by black thread.

The man examined them all in turn. "Three Cresidethians, a Takirov, two Nasaru and a half-breed – this is unusual. What is your purpose here in Senoja?" His voice was calm, and he spoke Nasaru with only a light accent.

Katonga had narrowed his eyes at being referred to as 'half-breed' but held his tongue.

Anyo answered. "We are travelling to Liialle."

"You are?" The leader tilted his head. "I see. Are you all singers, then?"

"No," he replied. "Those of us who have no talent are here as protection, as you can probably guess."

Behind him, it seemed Nuvin and his sisters exchanged a glance, but there was no way to alert everyone to his bluff. It was a half-truth in terms of their destination but above that, it was a foolish gamble. After all, who could sing amongst them? *But I've thrown the dice and I cannot share any more of the truth, either.*

"I wonder, could that last detail have been a threat?" The leader paused. "If so, that is a bold choice for strangers in our land."

"It is no insult, I swear as much," Anyo said. "Merely the

truth. We cannot all sing and in an unfamiliar place, it was only prudent to include guards."

One of the other soldiers had drawn his blade. "Makes me think of the sort of answer a spy might give. What do you think, Sivelii Jarnen?"

Jarnen nodded. "Perhaps a demonstration will allay our doubts."

Anyo turned to the group with a heaviness growing in his chest, but Binya was already walking forward, her expression one of calm.

"Allow me."

Binya straightened, then opened her mouth to sing. Takirov words flowed easily; her voice was husky but strong, and there was a lilting rhythm that added to the doubts held by the character in the lyrics. She only sang a single verse before stopping.

The leader raised an eyebrow. "Interesting indeed – few contralto performers compete; I might like to see you upon the stage, madam."

"Thank you," Binya replied with a smile.

Tension began to flow from Anyo's body. "I trust that this means –"

"Six of you to guard one singer does seem *exceptionally* prudent," the leader continued, his eyes roving across them once more. "Too prudent, even. And you must forgive me, madam, but you do not seem as though you are… quite wealthy enough to hire so many fine blades?"

"I'll take that as evidence of your diligence to your role rather than an insult," she replied.

Nuvin stood. "I believe I can satisfy your query, Sivelii."

Anyo hoped his eyes hadn't widened too much.

But when Nuvin sang, his voice rang across the ruin – and this time Anyo did not understand the words, but the tone was clear and there was a rousing element to what was again, only a short performance.

Jarnen spread his hands. "I admit that *two* singers might indeed seek plenty of protection on a long journey. However, I believe you will indulge me a moment by staying put while I converse with my fellow patriots."

"Of course," Anyo said.

While Jarnen took a small number with him some distance into the ruins, the rest of the soldiers remained at watch. All were yet to draw weapons, but nor did their grim expressions ease.

"A fine gambit," Binya said to Anyo, speaking Takirova. "I can see how you'd expect that I might be able to sing, but really, do you know how lucky you are?"

He grinned but it was as much bravado as relief. "I only hope such luck holds."

CHAPTER 16. – ROKURA

Dawn was quicker than Princess Kiteka's forces, reaching the cliff-side lair of the Duke first. But more importantly, the growing daylight had also been swifter than the mammoth. And Bedoa was definitely inside, according to Rokura's disc, which he had not seen for some time.

He stared across the plain from where he knelt upon grass, looking down at the enemy position. The stretch of land between them was free of dust for the moment, but a vibration travelled the earth. To feel the creature's approach from such a distance... would it smash through the very cliffs and tumble into the turmoil of the ocean?

Black waves chewing at the shoreline were somewhere out of view for now. From the hilltops above they would be clear, but not from Kiteka's position in the trees.

The lair was not so hidden, however. It was a fortified position built into a steep hillside, but one cloaked in the decay of age. When Rokura accepted the eyeglass from a Greyshield, it was clear that beneath the worn stone and grey wood of small doors and window frames were new bolts and steel plates. And within the windows that appeared dark and empty, painted steel mesh. An old trick once used in Takirov, to make a place seem abandoned from a distance, though not one that held up under close scrutiny.

He lowered the glass.

Almost difficult to believe that now, after such a long chase, Brutan was within reach. Depending on who exactly waited inside. *And Fara, if you're still alive, I will do my best.*

Asaro Itonye too, needed to be rescued with the others.

Providing the place wasn't simply a supply dump of heart-leaf or some other contraband.

"It would be folly to charge such a location without this so-called Stone Mammoth, wouldn't it?" one of the soldiers was saying, arms folded as he stared across at the lair.

"Exactly," someone answered. "We don't even know their numbers."

The Greyshield, her eyes holding a fair share of weariness, was also nodding along. "Sneaking in at night would be a better choice."

"That's not an option now," the first soldier said. "I heard one of the Viareya guys say the mammoth will keep smashing at that place until it finds what it wants, even if it takes days."

"If they have locals helping them in there, wouldn't the Duke know about the threat of Stone Mammoths?"

A different voice responded. "Supposedly. Exactly when the creatures will strike is hard to predict."

The rumbling in the earth grew stronger.

At the mouth of another road, a huge shape appeared from a cloud of growing dust.

Stone and earth cracked as the creature charged toward the lair, thunderous steps rumbling. Descriptions of its bulk had not been exaggerated. Easily as large as claimed, a mane of black scales covered half its body; stony, grey skin mottled with pale dust. The large head was dominated by a ridged brow that almost buried its burning eyes, pin-points of green, bright even from a distance.

"Look at how it moves," a soldier said, voice soft.

Rokura found his grip had tightened on one of his knives. The soldier was right; it was no clumsy beast, not at all frantic with a taste for whatever mineral it sought. Instead, it bore a singular drive, a purpose.

But he eased his grip. Some fortune still lingered around his life, having been ordered to accompany the princess *after* the vanguard was to make its attack.

Murmurs from the group fell silent as the Stone Mammoth neared the wall.

It lowered its head and struck. A punishing crack echoed across the plain, barely quieter when it reached him. Hunks of stone burst from the hillside, crashing to the ground at the creature's feet and leaving an enormous opening, cracks shooting through the cliff-face. Distant cries of terror and pain and rallying calls to attack alike drifted across the space as arrows, javelins, and stones were hurled down at the creature, most of which seemed to have little effect.

The beast continued to smash at the opening, a deep grunting following.

Princess Kiteka rose, Edazol at her side. "Remember our task here. Find Asaro, capture Bedoa."

Then she set off at a run.

Her force followed, all save for Feboa and one of his fellows. The man looked to Rokura. "Holding back?"

Rokura shook his head. "Ensuring my escort is ready."

"Get moving."

He suppressed a smile as he did, slipping between the grey trunks and setting off across the plain to where the battle continued, and where their vanguard would soon send a hail of projectiles at the creature's rear, hoping to make it turn and expose its face and eyes.

Kiteka signalled their approach, giving the Stone Mammoth wide berth. As expected, they received no fire on their approach to the barricaded entry off to the side, set deep within the stone. Once gathered before the door, a sorcerer placed some Coral on a hinge, its texture obviously changed somehow, now able to cling. *This is nothing I have seen before.*

The sorcerer motioned for everyone to take a step back. He placed his hands upon the Coral, which began to spread. It moved through the wood and steel alike, shimmering darkly as it did. Next, the man lifted a hammer.

He swung hard, shattering the door.

"Inside, now," Edazol commanded.

The sorcerer fell back, dropping to one knee, seemingly exhausted, as the princess and her soldiers charged into the lair.

Rokura drew his blades and followed.

Uneven light filled the corridors, lamps and torches spaced few and far between as they passed empty rooms. Dust filtered down from above, as the crashing of the Stone Mammoth continued, muffled shouts reaching them easily.

At the first set of stairs, the princess waved a small group ahead to finish checking the ground floor.

On the first floor, a pair of Takirov rebels stumbled into view, packs upon their back, provisions in hand. Steel flashed and both fell to lie motionless upon the stone floor. The princess drew them on, now switching to hand-signals for communication as yet again, a smaller group split off while she continued her ascent.

Large areas of light filled the third floor, dust swirling across broken bodies, some in shadow, others half-buried in rubble. Blood covered the floor and some of the walls, frantic footprints smeared within. Most of the surviving rebels, joined by Viareya men with their axes and hammers, fought the Stone Mammoth.

Rokura caught only a glimpse of the creature's massive, brutish face and searing eyes. Green blood was visible upon the creature's skin in trickles and smudges, the grunts it made much louder here.

But no-one wasted their good fortune by stopping to watch.

In the passages ahead, frantic whispers reached them. A familiar figure stepped into the light then, followed by a handful of Nasaru soldiers – Duke Bedeo. His usual expression of thinly-veiled contempt for everything before him had been replaced by wide eyes, his hair dishevelled and his cloak across one shoulder only.

He fled down one set of stairs without fully taking in his surroundings.

"We will deal with Bedeo," Edazol said, motioning for half the remaining force to pursue the traitor.

Which left a significantly reduced group to accompany the princess.

Kiteka turned to descend a second set of stairs, the chaos from above fading. They moved as swiftly as they could, sources of light just as irregular as before. It soon became clear that the stairs were winding far deeper than the ground level. They passed no doors or side passages but according to the princess, the disc suggested Brutan could be found below.

Which has to mean the prisoners, too.

And when the stone steps finally ended at a door, the muffled sound of young voices singing bled through the wood. The princess motioned for silence as she leant against the door to listen.

Rokura glanced at those beside him – Feboa and one other Greyshield.

Certainly a highly skilled group, but large numbers would be a problem if Brutan had filled the room beyond with soldiers too. And yet, what could explain the children singing? Hard to be certain, but the song sounded like it could have been Takirova.

"Eliminate any threats first," the princess said. "We cannot afford to lose Itonye."

"Have you ever seen the boy, Your Highness?" the other Greyshield asked.

"As a babe."

"It may be difficult to prioritise his life, depending on what we find within."

Rokura frowned. "Then we should attempt to save them all."

"I need not tell you that such a thing may not be possible." Kiteka lifted her blade. "Now, with me."

With her free hand, she turned the handle – unlocked – and burst inside.

Rokura dashed after, a harsh brightness giving him slight pause.

Lamps lined a broad, square chamber filled with seated

children. All wore the same warm-looking robe of brown. And while the children had been facing a small group of men before a board painted with Takirov words, the young ones spun with shocked cries at the princess' entry, their song ceasing.

Hopefully, one among them was Itonye, another Fara. *Either way, all are deserving of rescue.*

The largest man, with broad shoulders and stubbled cheeks – Brutan surely – waved an arm as he roared. "Stop them!"

Four rebels charged with weapons drawn.

Rokura let the others engage the four as he leapt between the children. Most were scrambling to duck under their desks, throwing themselves to the floorboards or scrambling for the corners.

He approached Brutan. The man's dark features were regular, but a cruel twist to his lips marred any possible kindness. It was, admittedly, odd to finally come face-to-face with someone he had chased so long, and never once seen clearly. "Your madness ends this day," Rokura said, speaking Takirova.

"A bold claim, stranger." Brutan threw his dark cloak back and lifted a heavy axe from his belt.

"Your lair is under attack by a Stone Mammoth. Bedoa and your allies are captured or dead by now – you could still surrender. Free these children."

Brutan raised an eyebrow. "Well, now. You do not sound quite like the typical king's dog."

And then the rebel leader leapt forward, axe whistling through the air.

Rokura twisted. Steel crashed into the flooring, splinters

flying. He slashed with his knives, tearing only through the edge of a sleeve. Brutan attacked again, a relentless pattern with huge backswings that nevertheless drove Rokura back, away from the clash of steel from behind, away from the whimpers and cries of the children.

When Rokura's back thumped against the wall, he ducked another swing – and this time, rolled forward to drive a blade into Brutan's foot. Rokura's other hand was already swinging down after, slamming a palm onto the pommel to pin his enemy.

Brutan grunted and his eyes burned as he lashed out in response, a meaty elbow knocking Rokura down. Despite the blurring to his vision, Rokura dropped his remaining blade and lifted both hands in time to catch Brutan's forearm.

The force nearly buckled his elbows, but it was enough to stop the axe.

"You're too old for this, Nasaru. You could be back there now, enjoying the ill-gotten fruits of Nasaru's nefarious past, but instead you chose to come here to die."

Rokura ground his teeth. "I disagree."

"Oh?"

"Yes," he replied. "For I know something that you do not."

Bloody steel burst through the man's chest.

Brutan gurgled as the strength in his arms vanished, pressure upon Rokura easing as the rebel leader fell to one knee. Rokura smacked the weapon from Brutan's grip and tore his knife free as he stood, looking down with a slight frown.

"You are in my debt, former Lord Rokura," Feboa said as he pushed Brutan over, the rebel lying face-down. Feboa used the man's cloak to wipe his blade clean.

"So it appears."

Sobbing from a dozen different voices filled the room – the sounds had probably never stopped – but now that the altogether contradictory silent-roar of battle had faded, Rokura could better notice it. Notice the small hands clinging to table legs or each other, to small, tear-streaked faces that peered around.

Other rebels were equally unmoving where they lay in pools of blood, along with the second Greyshield, but the princess stood unscathed beside the board and its Takirov song, sword in hand. She gazed across at the still-trembling children, her expression stern.

Kiteka raised her voice. "Asaro Itonye, we have come to save you."

Some of the sobbing eased.

Slowly, one of the older boys stood, and Rokura lowered his knives. Save for a tan complexion and brown hair, Asaro Itonye could have been a young man from Senoja. Or the village of Nokema.

CHAPTER 17. – ROKURA

Not only did the lad have blue eyes and light brown hair, but even his voice when he spoke sounded the way Rokura had imagined Iggy's might have. *Yet that is simply my own fanciful imagining.*

"I am he." Asaro's tone was wary as he glanced between Kiteka, Feboa and Rokura, then back to the princess. "And if you are truly here to save me, I hope you'll take us *all* away from this place."

"Of course." She approached with a smile, but she had not lowered her sword and the position of her arm suggested a firm grip…

Rokura frowned. Her actions made no sense. Did the princess actually mean to attack? He took half a step after her, but she was already lifting her weapon.

Feboa leapt between them, arms raised. "Your Highness, what is this?"

She exhaled. "This is me doing what I must, and if you do not stand aside you will join the little bastard."

"What?"

"Surely, I need not explain it to you? Asaro is a liability and

I will not allow my father to be blackmailed by the dregs of some Takirov rebels, nor the next lot who decide to use the secret against us." She pointed to Rokura without turning her head. "And now that I have you, the perfect scapegoat along for the journey, I will return with the very tragic news that a malcontent, former Lord Rokura, has sabotaged our mission."

Rokura straightened with a glare. So much of her behaviour made sense now – not merely the Hearing, the antagonism or the treatment as a prisoner, but being allowed to join her quest in the first place. Being kept close by, being taken directly to Asaro while Edazol was sent elsewhere. "Do not do this, Kiteka."

"Do not attempt to give *me* orders."

He pointed with one of his knives, moving toward Asaro. "You must know that I am not bound by your hierarchy."

She hissed as she swung, but Feboa blocked her – and all too quickly, they were locked in an exchange of feints and slashes. Lending aid to the Greyshield would be risky, but if he was careful…

Feboa gave ground to her somewhat longer reach, knocking into tables and chairs as he did. One of her swipes drew blood but Feboa twisted and kicked out, knocking her blow aside. The Greyshield followed up with a swing of a parrying dagger.

It was an overextension.

Kiteka lunged before Feboa could recover, her blade piercing his chest. He slumped forward – but though he shuddered, he spat a great spray of blood across her face.

She's blinded!

Rokura cast a dagger as he twisted around them. It thudded into her back and though she spun away with a grunt, she could not anticipate his next move. Nor could she trace the path of the second blade as he swung.

It crunched into the side of her neck.

Blood spurted free as he wrenched the knife deeper and shoved the princess to the floorboards. She thumped down and grew motionless awfully quickly, Feboa's body just as still where it lay nearby.

It seemed, quite suddenly, that everywhere Rokura looked, blood was pooling.

He exhaled, long and hard.

And now, an actual reason to Exile me.

Yet certain things should still be observed, shouldn't they?

Rokura knelt… and ended up wiping his hands and then his blades upon her cloak, ramming them back into their sheaths. *What had she become?* He closed the princess' empty eyes and began to position her hands upon her chest… and then let them fall free, the arrangement of peace unfinished. After all, what dignity was she owed?

Perhaps none. *Even with all the blood I have shed… I would not try to do what she has attempted here.*

He looked up at Asaro, who was approaching and whose jaw was clenched. The young man had not turned away; instead he'd obviously moved to shield some of the nearest children from the sight. "Lad, I assume you know why she tried to kill you?"

"I do."

"If I am able to bring everyone here out to safety, would you come with me to meet someone who might be able to help you?"

"I will follow you from this place, at least."

"Good enough for now." Rokura stood, then raised his voice. "The oldest among you, help the others prepare as best you can. Take some lamps. We are leaving. If any are hurt, bring them to me. I will carry any who need it."

And while it did seem that more than a few were bruised, and plenty still trembled as they moved, none had any serious injuries.

Aside from whatever scars their minds will have borne. What toll had such a scene – and everything else they must have witnessed in the weeks prior – taken upon their little lives? *And I have been a part of that suffering this day. I must atone.*

In the darkened stair, Rokura led with his blades free, Asaro close behind and one of the older children bringing up the rear. Most kept pace, but over time, about a third were being carried – from what seemed to be weariness, rather than wounds the young ones might not have been willing to mention before.

Upon reaching the halls above, a heavy quiet became apparent. The Mammoth was no longer attacking.

The hush remained unbroken and they faced no attack or even questions as he took the children past more bodies. So, too, when he ascended eventually to the passage leading free of the lair, and even when he drew them across the plain with only a single backward glance to where Captain Ovedi and the survivors worked to harvest the Stone Mammoth, swinging axes with grunts of effort. *Impressive.*

He did not notice Edazol there, but that didn't mean the man had perished.

The same of which could be said of the duke.

But the thought had to be set aside when he reached the

tree line, where the rear guard and horses waited. There, he explained a version of events within the lair, claiming that the princess had sent him out with the others, and that Kiteka herself had told him she had to be the one to bring Asaro back.

The soldiers did not so much as bat an eyelid at his claim. *If nothing else, her behaviour is easy to predict.*

He asked them to check upon his charges and permitted himself a moment for water. Next, he moved between the older children with a smile, asking after Fara, only to learn nothing. *Then a cruel fate has already befallen him?*

At the very least, some of the children were now beginning to murmur to each other in tones of relief.

He let them be then, moving away with some relief of his own.

Asaro approached, lowering his voice. "You have done as you claimed. I will listen to what you have to say."

"Good. My name is Rokura; former lord and Greyshield," he said.

"Former?"

"That is a long story. I had worked directly for the king for some years, yet I know little about your life. And even had I been given some lengthy report, I would not claim to understand whatever you have suffered, what happiness might have been taken from you."

The young man nodded, perhaps in appreciation.

"But I still ask that you believe I wish to help you," he added. "And to that end, I have a question that might seem odd. Would you tell me, what do you know of the Inora people?"

Asaro's eyebrows lifted. "Interesting. You do not take me for having Senoja blood."

"Perhaps not."

"Then, are you offering to take me to the village of Nokema?"

The young man's knowledge was more detailed than others, since so many had seemed to have forgotten the Inora. Yet if Asaro's mother had been an Exile, or perhaps someone who fled Iggy's home in the past, it was no surprise he would want to return.

Equally, if Asaro did share lineage with the Senoja, that too might be a simple explanation of his knowledge. "If I can. But the person I believe can help may not be there right now. He may be in Takirov."

"Who is this person?"

"Iggy. He is a few years younger than you but he may even know your mother or extended family? Although, I am wondering, perhaps, as much as guessing." He paused. *No use getting ahead of myself, I know nothing about his young man.* "But Iggy's mind; he is one of the most powerful people I have met. If any could help you avoid the king's reach, should you wish it, then I believe it is Iggy of the Inora."

"You mean, unlike me, this Iggy has the gift?"

"He does have a gift, yes."

Asaro glanced back toward the cliff-side lair, staring for some time. His face revealed nothing about what he might be thinking. "The connection to my father was not the only thing the rebels wanted me for. They wanted to twist all of our minds for some purpose… but when they eventually confirmed that I *was* Asaro Itonye, they spoke of bringing in Sun-Killers to 'dig out' my gift, if I ended up not being as useful as they hoped."

"I can only say that it seems most fortunate you avoided such a fate," Rokura said. Nothing from the war or more recent clashes suggested such a thing was at all common, yet who knew what the Sun-Killers were capable of. "It sounds as though blackmailing the king was their first goal."

"It was." Asaro sighed. "And so it might be my own, now."

Rokura hesitated. "… you wish to blackmail your father?"

"He deserves no such honorific."

"That I can certainly understand, but if freedom is your goal, could you not take it without retaliation?"

"For myself?" He shrugged. "Perhaps. But not for my siblings."

"You do not mean…"

"Not the royals, no. I mean other bastards. Three that my mother told me of."

Rokura exhaled. "And she was certain?"

"She met the other women he used."

"I see." Once more, it seemed the work of protecting a young man, someone who found themselves far from their home, would fall to an old man. *In truth, not a terrible use for whatever remains of my life. Oyo would certainly approve.* Rokura extended his hand.

Asaro accepted the handshake. "I appreciate your offer, and I hope you can help me as promised."

"I will."

"And you can convince this Iggy from Nokema to help us?"

He smiled. "That may not be so easy, but when we find him, he will listen."

"You make him sound stubborn."

"Another facet to his strength."

"Good," the young man replied, and smiled for the first time.

CHAPTER 18. – IGGY

For all his hesitation, there was little to think about – he had no choice. If Mei really was in danger and the Mistress telling the truth, then crossing the range at speed was vital. He could not use the rays of the sun to visit a place he had not known, and the Mistress had made it clear that whoever travelled with Mei would prevent Iggy from using Mei herself as an anchor.

And so when darkness cloaked the mountain peaks at last, Iggy rose with a frown and a growing weariness.

What must I do?

Hold on to your consciousness as long as you can – use us to do so. Once we land on the other side, you will need to find specific information, but know that we will guide you.

That doesn't explain what –

Iggy stiffened at a new heaviness in his limbs, as though stones had been attached to his body. His torso was next and he crumbled to the ground, head following like a boulder that strained his neck until it too – until everything – reached the earth and then seemed to *sink* further, too much for even the ground to contain.

He tried to move but even his heartbeat was slowing as a

true dark followed.

Scraps of white and grey lingered in his vision like twisting scarves and he clutched for each one, clinging to the only point of difference left in his mind.

Good, Iggy. Do not let go. Even Nuka's voice was muffled.

He kept his grip.

The darkness swirled, crushing him with waves, attacking in a rhythm that allowed just enough time to steel himself for the next. It was not enough to break him. He clenched his fists tighter as the sisters dragged him along, the vague sense of movement very faint. As though a blur of treetops and stony peaks flowed beneath him… and the agony grew.

The shadow-waves pressed down harder, far too hard.

Each swirl of light became like smoke between his fingers but he did not stop grasping.

Focus only on us.

Iggy did as instructed by Itula, grunting at another pummelling from the shadow.

Their flight continued, tearing at his body.

How much longer?

Two more peaks, that is all.

But the darkness was bleeding into the white and the grey, and soon there was but a single speck that no matter how much he stretched toward, he could no longer touch.

***

When Iggy woke, it was to blessed light.

And he was looking down, walking upon a street lined with wooden boards, each polished and fitted together neatly. He glanced up. It was not a harbour. More importantly, it was not a mountain range! *Wait, where am I?*

The sisters did not answer.

Around him, the houses stood in a uniform dark stone, yet the tiles upon some rooves might have been painted bright colours, considering the range of grey. Round windows featured flower-boxes and beside doorways, small, sculpted trees planted in pots rose up. Some bore little nuts with two distinct shades, almost like cats eyes... and children ran throughout the streets collecting them, laughing and smiling while parents looked on from the steps.

And everyone familiar-looking; it could have been a scene from Nokema... though there were differences. Instead of cross stitching, the tunics and robes were stitched in such a way as to appear almost like an ululating serpent, and the rhythm of the language was a little faster, though many words were similar, or even the same.

One striking difference could be found in the pair of soldiers he saw, with their graceful, silver circlets and more, breastplates and other pieces quite pale but covered in a gauze that was darker... not at all war-like, in that sense. But they still carried bows and narrow swords.

Even so, neither seemed close to using their weapons. The two simply stood together at a merchant's shopfront, drinking from steaming mugs.

Above the building rested a sign with somewhat familiar letters. And while he'd not actually have been able to read them, Inora or otherwise, Iggy slowed to examine the markings – only he did not slow at all, let alone stop.

His feet continued down the street.

And finally, finally, he realised what should have been obvious from the moment he regained consciousness.

I'm not controlling my body!

Not only that, but neither the children, the soldiers nor other people passing in the street gave him a second look.

They only see what I want them to see.

Nuka, are you controlling me too?

No, that would be Vija. I'm confusing the minds of the Senoja and Itula is searching for your sister's trail. It's easier to find, now that we're so much closer.

Vija? Closer? I... I need to stop. Iggy fought against the forward motion of his body, but he couldn't bring himself to a halt, couldn't even cause a single stumble.

There was a neat little garden ahead, where children played and adults sat eating and talking in small groups.

His body took him to a wooden bench that had been carved to resemble a more friendly Blood Cat, positioned in a somewhat out of the way part of the garden, where he was forced to sit. At least no-one else was nearby to observe him, but then, perhaps that was exactly what the sisters had in mind.

Let's take a moment.

There had better not be a fourth sister in here with me. He wanted to fold his arms but that wasn't possible. *I want an explanation, Nuka.*

Of course. You know Vija as the Mistress, but we hardly call her that, as you can imagine.

Italu chuckled. Maybe we should – she can be quite pushy.

That's enough, ladies. Iggy, here is what happened – do follow along, as I won't repeat myself.

He tried and failed to nod, needless as the gesture would have been.

After crossing the mountain range, you lost consciousness.

However, despite surviving the passage, you could not wake. You were close to death and we had landed near a village – too near to be safe. In order to avoid the chance of you being captured or worse, we took command of your limbs, and brought you here to Hiila. It is close to Kaarsi, which I believe Itula can confirm is now also the location of your sister.

It is. And she is alive and well, for now.

An entirely reasonable explanation. But not a satisfactory one at all. *Give me back control over my body.*

When you are ready – you are quite fast to heal, so merely another day, by my estimation.

I'm ready now!

It only seems that way because we are helping you.

If you do not believe us, I will loosen my hold.

Despite how childish it would have been, the urge to stamp his foot was strong – they had no right! And so he asked, and without any consideration as to what that might mean. *Show me, then.*

So be it.

Darkness clawed its way back into his body.

CHAPTER 19. – IGGY

At the edge of the small city of Hiila, the sisters directed him across a yard of dirt toward the nearest beast of burden – it was a strange animal with short feathers of metallic grey and another, darker shade. Its head was pointed, with keen eyes resting upon a long neck. Legs and clawed feet alike gave an impression that the beast might have been close to some sort of lizard, but it was not so slender; being quite solid, without giving off an unwieldy air.

And when the animal at the head of the line, laden with two passengers and their baggage, let out a clacking cry and dashed from the yard into the plain, Iggy added 'swift' to his list of descriptions.

No surprise. The sisters were seeking speed. *Aren't I too? If Mei really is so close, along with whoever is keeping her prisoner...* And considering his failure to fully recover, Iggy was dependent upon the sisters, both to avoid a return to blackness *and* to do almost everything else, for that matter.

One of the handlers approached, an older man with a greying beard. "Ten silver squares to Kaarsi, lad."

Of course, here you are. Iggy's hand raised and though nothing dropped into the man's palm, the fellow nodded in satisfaction, as if he'd both heard the Mistress and received payment.

This isn't right.

Such deception is a small price for our futures.

"First time on a Tonil?" the man asked as he led Iggy over to the next animal.

Iggy nodded. Or, Vija nodded for him.

"I'll help you into the saddle," the man offered, lifting Iggy up and getting him settled, placing the leather reins into his hands. "Now, you keep a hold of these, as he'll move quickly."

Right.

"Even if you lose them at one point, he knows where to go. Just don't fall off, as there're no refunds."

I understand.

"Good. Now, fast as they are, they can't run forever. There're two stops between here and the Kaarsi, so take that time for a meal and stretch your legs or whatever." The man patted the creature's neck, and it offered a purring sound in response. "He'll call to you when he's rested himself – there are places for them to drink and feed; the Tonil know what to do, so you don't need to worry."

This is all quite impressive.

He grinned. "We're the best Tonil service in all the land – you're benefiting from generations of experience."

The Mistress used Iggy to point at a collar set with black coral. And a little sorcery?

"Never turn down a useful tool."

Oh?

"The collars allow us to call them back if they get lost, you see." Another pair of travellers approached from the huge wooden gates of Hiila. "Now, if you're ready, just tap his flanks, as I'd best see to these fine customers."

Iggy did so, a little smack ringing from the hard feathers – or were they actually scales? The Tonil leapt forward with a clacking that vibrated, claws kicking up dust as it picked up speed.

Wind buffeted Iggy's face as swaying grass and more dirt upon the plains rolled by. It might have been an exhilarating ride if not for his lack of control. The urge to grip the reins tighter was frustrated by Vija's own hold, which *was* firm, at least.

But even the inability to clench his legs a little more, or to decide what to focus on…

There *was* one thing that she seemed interested in: when the Tonil's path ran parallel with a paved road, and it became clear neither horse nor carriage could keep pace.

Things have certainly changed while we waited.

Waited?

Yes.

She did not elaborate and he did not bother asking; she wouldn't have shared anyway.

When they reached the first stop, appearing exactly like a wide pen with two open gates, he was glad to dismount – under Vija's direction, of course. Troughs of water and what seemed to be piles of roots were positioned around the enclosure, and while the Tonil had come to a smooth halt, its clacking sounds were impatient. And when it went directly to the water and plunged its head within, that confirmed his impression.

I need water too, he told the sisters, and Vija moved him across the space and dunked his own head into one of the free troughs.

Cool enveloped him, and a slight, metallic taste was the only drawback to quenching his thirst.

That's enough. I should sun-bathe now.

Vija made him straighten, then took him to the fence before removing his shirt and then leaning him back against the wood, its grains uneven against his skin. Next, the three started yet another conversation in their private language, lowered to a murmur that he was able to ignore as he let the light soothe him.

The passing of time grew slower, or unclear, but when the Tonil's call reached him, Iggy soon found himself back in the saddle, racing across the plain.

Later still, when their path drew nearer to the highway once more, and he was able to watch them again, it really was obvious just how easily the creatures could outpace the few horses he saw. *Why doesn't everyone use the Tonils here?*

Nuka answered. They are not large in number, it seems, and owned by only the oldest merchant families. Few others know how to rear them, let alone train the Tonils.

Ah.

Ahead, a large wood rose from the horizon. The edges were marked by hints of old walls, half-tumbled, stone worn down by wind and rain. The Tonil would reach it and the second pen soon; it was already starting to slow. Which was pleasing enough, considering the growing ache in his muscles.

Do you sense that? Itula asked. I think someone is waiting in the woods with mischievous intent.

From her tone, it did not seem like a true threat, but why else would she have warned everyone? *An enemy? Waiting for us?*

Of course. So-called Sun-killers, led by a Silent One.

A Silent One?

Surely you know of them? Silent Ones were bred in order to nullify power such as yours and to hunt rogue Sun-Killers, among other things. They, like the Tonil, are few in number.

You are stronger, Iggy.

What about each of you? If it is a large group with this Silent One, won't I need some help?

Possibly, but I do not imagine so. It sounded as though she were smiling. The problem will be the attention you draw after using your gifts.

I will handle that, sister. Nuka sounded more firm than usual.

Familiar frustration built but he kept his voice even. *Then I must be ready to have control of my body again.*

He's probably right. Sisters?

Their agreement echoed within his mind.

A tingling in both hands followed, then his feet and legs, climbing his thighs and swirling down from his arms at the same time, until his entire body seemed more alive than before, and once more under his command.

Iggy clenched his legs around the saddle, reins in hand, searching the trees ahead with his mind. How wonderful it was to actually choose where to focus! But what he found revealed nothing about the waiting Sun-Killers. A pair of birds took flight, but that was all.

It wasn't until shade from the trees fell across him, bringing a shiver, leaves flying by, that the sense waiting power reached him. Nowhere to be seen yet, but even combined, it did not seem to rival many from back home. The Mistress was right... *Am I that much stronger because I'm from Nokema? Because of Father?*

Many of the strongest were sent away as Guardians.

There will be time for that later. The Mistress did hold a note of concern in her dark voice. **It is the Silent One you will have to be careful with. No direct strikes, understand?**

The advice but not the reason.

For now, that is enough.

At a sharp curve in the path, the Tonil slowed, but Iggy still had to cling to its neck. The second pen appeared ahead, similar save for the dozen Sun-Killers in their white clothing, trimmed with something reflective, weapons not visible at a glance.

In their centre waited the Silent One. It seemed she was a young woman and she wore black, with her entire head and face wrapped in a grey scarf. Even her hands were hidden beneath gloves of a similar shade.

Iggy did not give her further attention, as psychic blows from the Sun-Killers were already crashing against him.

Yet they were easy to withstand, like stinging gnats only.

He lashed out with a blast of his own.

All fell to the dirt, stunned, breathless or perhaps even dead, though he had tried not to simply slaughter them.

The Silent One made no move to attack in response – no move at all.

As the Tonil thudded to a halt, Iggy leapt down. He kept his feet well enough as he fell into a crouch and gathered his power... but not for a direct strike. Instead, he had to try something different. *What if I just tried to contain her?* Like the Paragons and other adults had sometimes done for little ones back home. *And all the while thinking they were hiding their method from the rest of us.*

And so he hurled down an invisible cage of power, using

it to prevent the Silent One from accessing her gift, for who knew what else she was capable of?

The Silent One's shoulders slumped.

Iggy rose and approached, slow steps only. She seemed to have given up completely, head resting against her chest. *Is this enough?*

Yes. Well done.

This was too easy, wasn't it? Iggy stopped a few feet away, close enough now to see that the Silent One was breathing hard… and that the scarf was damp… as if it had soaked up tears…

Only because we told you what to do. If you'd attacked directly, you would have suffered the strike yourself. Silent Ones absorb and reflect, and they are stronger for it when their other senses are dulled.

He shuddered. *But why didn't she protect the others?*

Simply, they cannot. Their power is only for themselves.

A new concern was growing. Could it be that whoever sent the Sun-Killers expected a blistering, raging attack? They knew exactly *who* they were seeking. Because any local would understand a Silent One, and what a direct attack would mean. *They know who I am… They know I'm from Nokema.*

That is most likely true, Itula said, curiosity in her voice.

Then who in Senoja knows who I am? And where *I am?*

Many would be aware of your power, and some obviously that you are Inora. However, none will lay a hand upon you so long as we are here.

Her words were of comfort, even if her tone was not so kind as Nuka's tended to be – it was the kind of thing Mei would have said. *Or what Mother* should *have said.*

"Please – I beg of you, stranger. Please save me."

The voice was soft and weary, and not at all distant. Iggy faced the so-called Silent One.

CHAPTER 20. – ANYO

Sivelii Jarnen had promised safe passage to the singing city of Liialle, and it seemed he and his score of soldiers would deliver.

It was also clear that their actions were not without hidden motives.

A suspicion Han was quick to bring up now, while taking a moment to eat from their dwindling supplies. They rested upon a grassy plain, taking advantage of shelter offered by spreading trees of green and gold. In that, they were one of several groups of travellers choosing to rest upon the plain as the sun began to set, settling not so far from the highway.

Liialle itself was quite close; the flow of travellers, merchants and farmhands led to tiered stone walls and a glimmering palace above. From its peaks rose coloured smoke – red, white and yellow – signalling the anniversary of the city's founding, if Anyo recalled correctly.

"Well, lad?" Han gave him a nudge.

"It might well be impossible to discover exactly what Jarnen wants until the moment is upon us," Anyo replied.

"Think we can afford that?"

"No." Anyo glanced over to where the Senoja leader spoke

with one of his seconds. "Want to see if we can make him reveal his hand?"

Han lowered his voice. "How so?"

"Thank him for the help, then let him know that we're parting ways here – we're quite close to the city, and he isn't pressing on for some reason. If the man attempts to stop us, we have confirmation of that much, at least."

"That either provokes our capture or a fight," Han said.

"Or, he lets us go and sends someone to tail us, once we're inside the city."

"Aye, that I can imagine too. Maybe." Han rubbed at his stubble. "Very well, your little gamble paid off before; let's hope this one does too."

"Tell the others we're leaving, but not to rush. I don't want the soldiers to misinterpret any of our actions."

"You're telling him now?"

Anyo nodded. "Best not to delay it. I think we'll need what's left of the daylight to find lodgings, anyway. I don't remember exactly what conditions are like for foreigners this far west, even in a large place like Liialle."

"Assuming we can pass the gates. It might be easier to have the escort at least a little longer, you know."

"True, but I think Nuvin may just have the answer there."

"If he's really a monk and a diplomat."

Anyo grinned. "Finding it hard to trust even our allies, I see."

"That's what kept me alive for all these years."

"Then you know the Femithir have visited the palace before. He is what he seems."

"Probably," the older man said, giving Anyo a pat upon the back. "Go on then."

Anyo approached Jarnen as Han spoke to the others. "Sivelii Jarnen, we wish to thank you for your kindness in escorting us to Liialle."

The fellow smiled, but its warmth did not reach his eyes. "I could not have our hospitality called into question, you see."

"We are in your debt."

Jarnen waved a hand. "No debt is accepted, but I would offer some advice. Should you find yourself in the eastern streets, seek out an inn by the name of the Soaring Flag. It welcomes even Nasaru folk, and is but a short walk to the amphitheatre."

"That is most welcome. Thank you again, Sivelii."

And then they were simply collecting their belongings and setting off toward the Singing City, no longer surrounded by silent soldiers with eyes narrowed in suspicion or distaste.

"That was easy enough." Katonga glanced over his shoulder and offered a wave that seemed wholly insincere.

"They will follow us, surely," Nuvin said.

"And I'll bet everything I have on that Soaring Flag place being filled to the ceiling with spies," Han added.

"Fortunately, I can arrange for sparse but more private lodgings," Nuvin said. "Though I have no doubt we will be watched anywhere we go."

"Then we won't tarry in Lialle," Anyo replied.

Binya frowned. "Only if we find something to lead us to Misha's grave. And only if she took the sword with her."

"Worries I admit I do share." He could not keep a sudden weariness from his voice. Hope and excitement had vanished, just as she'd warned. Not even escaping the clutches of Jarnen – for now, at least – was enough to stave off fresh doubts. There was a mountain before him. *And I am little more than an ant.*

"They are fair," she said. "We are no longer searching quiet places at our leisure for the clues we need. We are going to be watched and possibly hunted if something goes wrong."

"Meaning that you expect us to be here for longer than we wish."

"It seems certain."

He nodded, because of course she was right. And glancing at the growing concern on everyone else's faces, it was no surprise. "Then clearly we need something more than what we have in mind for the Singing City. A new method, a new idea, *something*."

"Got any, lad?"

"Perhaps." But it was nothing sophisticated – merely the possibility of checking records for mention of past entrants. If nothing else, it would prove that Rinbe's wife had visited Liialle. "First, we need to pass the gate. Nuvin, can you deliver on your promise?"

"I absolutely can."

Anyo managed a small smile. "Good."

CHAPTER 21. – ANYO

Nuvin brought the small group to a halt before lodgings which were not so close to the amphitheatre at all, but which appeared warm and welcoming, at least.

It was not simply the cleanliness of the place. Nor the scent of fresh flowers inside, but the smiles with which they were greeted by Cresidethians. Some wore similar robes to Nuvin, though just as many were attired in yellow pants and black shirts.

Unlike a tavern in Nasaru, there was no long bench in the common room. Instead, a large, circular column of wooden panels waited in the centre of the floor. From it, servers brought out drinks and steaming plates of spiced pork, using multiple openings around the circle.

And from behind the nearest server, set half a floor below, Anyo caught a glimpse of flames and flashing knives. The cooks at work, it seemed.

One of the workers met and escorted them to pair of tables, where Anyo found himself seated at the smaller one with Binya and Katonga. For a time, while they ate their own spiced meals and Binya took more of the sweet lorimir, it was almost possible to forget about precisely how naïve hope had made him…

After the meal, the servers showed everyone to their lodgings – accessed from a dark hallway. The wooden doors revealed small rooms which were, like the kitchen, set 'down' in the fashion of other villages and towns in Senoja. Another sign of Cresidethians adapting to the local buildings, no doubt.

Adapted or not, the place was clean and warm, with rugs upon the floors *and* hanging upon the walls.

It wasn't until he sat on the bed that he noticed another detail courtesy of twin lamps – a dark board leant against the wall, with stubs of coloured chalk upon a sill. For… visiting children to use? A thoughtful place.

Yet he had barely thrown himself back across the sheet before rising again. *I need more space.*

Anyo left his door ajar, since it bore no lock but instead a bolt of wood, and paced the hallway. Except, it was not so much *pacing* as moving quietly to one end and pausing to think for a time, so as not to disturb anyone's sleep before heading back toward his room and pausing again.

But no solutions came. No new, brilliant ideas.

Each pause grew longer and longer, until he found himself simply staring at a pattern of stone in the wall – it could have been a praying mantis. *And if you're thinking about that, you're not thinking about anything useful at all, are you?*

Soft footsteps approached.

Binya.

"You seem restless." She stopped before him, her expression difficult to read once more. "Shouldn't you try sleeping?"

He chuckled. "And yourself?"

"I need a little less – I'm not the leader here."

Anyo leant against the wall. "Leader, huh? If so, I suspect I need to do a lot better."

She joined him. "Then do exactly that – just do it in the morning."

"Is that a solicitous comment or a rebuke?"

"I'm not here to drag you down with your mistakes – in fact, I'm not even sure you've made that many. We're all still following you, and it's not as though we've failed here in Senoja, either."

He straightened a little as she continued.

"You're fortunate to have me and the others around you, fortunate to have reached the Singing City unscathed. So you have a responsibility to take advantage of that good fortune, not to squander it on doubts."

"That is an interesting perspective… I would like to believe it."

Binya gripped his arm. "Do so. And another thing. You should know that we are not expecting you to solve everything with perfect grace. Only *you* seem to be placing that weight upon your own shoulders all of a sudden, Your Highness."

Anyo blinked down at the woman. Was she right? There was a fierceness to her gaze now, as if she could compel him to believe her words. To believe in himself.

And she was standing very close.

I hadn't even noticed…

She wore only an undershirt that left her smooth arms bare, most of her legs also – and up close, the flecks of hazel in her eyes drew him near. Her lips too, if he leant a little nearer…

Binya released his arm, but she was smiling. "Follow me."

She was already halfway to his room, where she gestured

for him to enter. Inside, Binya closed the door and slid the wooden bolt home. Then, she moved to the lamps, where she blew one out, the scent of smoke hanging in the air a moment.

Binya closed the distance between them and took his face into her hands, her lips so near to his now. "Here is one moment where you need not worry about what you truly desire, I hope."

Anyo wrapped his arms around her waist, her skin warm beneath the fabric. Even such a simple but wonderful act caused a tingling throughout his body. "This, I am sure of."

Their lips met. He closed his eyes as he pulled Binya back onto the bed. She broke their kiss to run her lips along his neck, the scent of her hair enveloping him.

He ran his hands across her back, sliding down to her thighs and she bit into his skin in response; he could almost feel her grin.

Time had slowed.

Wonderfully so.

Anyo sank into the moment, tension and doubt vanishing as the room grew darker, smaller, more intimate; his mind singularly focused on the softness of her hands as she urged him to a half-sitting position to lift his tunic free, flinging her own undershirt to the bed in almost the same movement.

She drew him to her, nipples pressed against his chest and once more, her mouth and tongue sought his own.

And finally, he did not need to think at all.

***

Morning light streaming through the window drew Anyo from the bed and he swung his feet free of the blanket… and found himself very naked. "Oh."

He glanced over his shoulder to where Binya lay sleeping beside him, breathing softly, her face half-pressed into the pillow, so that her nose was a little twisted. Anyo smiled as he rose, pulling his clothes on with a certain extra energy to his movements.

Even when drinking from his flask, he had to navigate a grin.

My whole body… this is better. So much of his doubt had been banished. The problems of the day could be met, and if not surmounted at once; there was no reason to accept defeat.

"You seem a little more sprightly."

Binya was pulling her clothing back on.

He lowered the flask. "Obviously, I have you to thank for that."

She ran both hands through her short hair and stretched. "Let's join the others for breakfast then, before they start to miss us."

"Together?"

"Of course," she replied with a chuckle. "They won't know what we did, if that's what you're thinking."

He shrugged. "You know, I'm not sure what I'm thinking."

"Then let me get to my room so I can pack," she said.

When he reached the common room, there was only one other traveller, a young woman who drank from water that had been left upon a shelf in the serving column. Quite a number of other glasses stood untouched. Enough for each patron?

Movement drew his gaze – Katonga at one of the larger tables, everyone ready to leave, it seemed. *Except me and Binya, that is.*

"We've been talking while you luxuriated," Kat said. "And we've come up with a simple idea, but it has its risks."

He took a seat. "I'm listening."

"We split up. Han and I take Elin and Fiana to the library while you, Nuvin and Binya visit the amphitheatre. After all, they are the singers. You could even register to compete – to keep up appearances for Jarnen and his men. This way, at least, we cover more ground quickly."

"We would," Anyo said with a nod. Several questions followed, since as Katonga admitted, risks were involved. "We might all be in more danger, divided. Jarnen would not need many extra swords, if any, to capture us, or worse."

Katonga was nodding.

"And if we do head directly to the amphitheatre, can we even afford to pay for entry?"

"The competition is open to all. The entry is a test of voice, not of connections or wealth," Nuvin said as Binya approached and joined their table.

"What have I missed?" she asked and though she glanced at everyone, her gaze did not linger anywhere. She was behaving exactly as promised; her usual self.

Katonga explained and she nodded. "Would we return here if pursued? Flee the city?"

"Perhaps," Nuvin replied. "What leniency is offered to this place would be stretched. The owner would help us escape, if nothing else."

"Preventing Jarnen from learning our true purpose, from deciding to capture us, is something we have to deal with," Han said. "If so, we'll have a better chance of a proper search."

"Can't we do both?" Elin asked.

"How?"

"By leading them on a wild goose chase. When we leave the

library, we'll distract them," she said. "Draw whoever follows us to away from the amphitheatre."

"It's worth a try, if you are willing," Anyo said.

Nods followed.

"Good. Who leads the city now?" Anyo asked. "I do not recall, but would the Master of Liialle help you, considering your diplomatic status?"

Nuvin shook his head after a moment's thought. "Unlikely. Granted I have only visited Liialle twice before, but Irgav is a former general and hero of the previous two wars. He would likely be just as suspicious as Jarnen himself."

"Ah. If it's still Irgav, then I agree. He may even recognise me, since he has visited the palace before," Anyo said with a sigh. "I believe we will risk splitting up. Any final suggestions?"

Han seemed about to speak, but he did not. And when everyone gathered their possessions and stood, Nuvin and his sisters taking Binya to explain about the water, Katonga was the one to voice concern. "Is there another way to do this, Anyo?"

"Save for slinking around at night in an unfamiliar city, I cannot think of one."

He sighed. "I might be able to move more freely alone, if you want me to undertake something that's best described as an even greater risk."

Anyo hesitated, certain he had guessed the man's suggestion. He shook his head. "Targeting sergeant Jarnen is too far. If you were caught, or the murder traced back to us, we would be executed at best. As things stand now, should Jarnen make a move, we might only be expelled as spies."

"I suppose that is true."

Han took Anyo by the shoulders. "You know my oath, lad. And if I end up playing decoy, if that is really the best way to keep that oath – and if it's your wish – I'll play that part. But only if you are certain."

He smiled. "Thank you, Han. And I don't believe we have much choice. The sooner we find another clue and leave, the better."

"Aye, the sooner the better."

CHAPTER 22. – ANYO

"Nuvin, what do the animals say now?" Anyo asked as they detoured a group of workers. The men and women were bent over a patch of usually smooth boards that covered a magnificent square, which in turn granted access to the towering amphitheatre. They were replacing a fairly large section of boards, patches of sweat growing across their smocks even as Anyo passed.

Nearby, an overseer leant against a cart, drinking from his flask. His own clothes were free of any sign of exertion.

Nuvin tilted his head… perhaps in the direction of robins flitting about from branches that hung over the walls of a nearby merchant. At least for now, the animals were speaking to him again. Did it have anything to do with the personal risk he'd taken in the Sky Carriage? "Nothing has changed. We're still being followed – a pair of them. One street back now; they know where we're going, it seems."

And while the birds were not precisely necessary to confirm that soldiers – and citizens too – took an interest in their movements through the streets, confirmation from the robins was not without value. What *was* disappointing was their lack of clear knowledge about Misha.

She could have been any one of the various foreign singers the birds had mentioned to Nuvin.

Which still left the amphitheatre as their best hope, for now.

It was an imposing but still graceful construction.

Three types of stone rose up; dark, glittering granite at the base – the majority of the walls themselves, actually. Next came marble and finally, along the top, a far smaller row of blue and white quartz, almost like clean-cut spikes of a palisade.

At the base, wide stairs flanked an open entryway. If not for ornate steel gates, would the stairs have permitted access to seating? Inside, similar gates and stairs descended, but walls in the entryway were quite bare.

Round windows let plenty of light within, falling across a young man in a blue vest. His clothing was almost military in design, but no weapons were visible where he stood in the marble reception-area, waiting behind a bench of dark marble. He straightened with a small sound of surprise or perhaps guilt, adjusting the collar upon his coat as he did. "Ah, welcome to the Songbird Theatre. Are you here to register? I must warn you, the competition does not begin for over a month."

"Perhaps not me," Anyo said with a smile, his Senoja coming easily enough despite a long stretch between when he'd last used it. "My friends are far more gifted when it comes to singing. We have come to ask, if it is possible to perhaps find inspiration in the contestants?"

"There is a small library of such stories here, of course. Busts of past champions can also be found in the halls to your left… unless you mean recent champions? Eedija still resides in the city and runs a successful school, for example."

"I think seeing or reading about any who have come before us would be wonderful," Nuvin said. It seemed he, too, was able to speak Senoja. *That shouldn't be a surprise, considering his role.*

The fellow gestured to the arch to his right. "Please, take whatever time you need."

The hallway also featured potted plants flowing yellow and pink, and while the busts bore names and dates of victories, Anyo found himself squinting at the words or pausing to take a little extra time to read.

"That one is Hejann," Nuvin said. "The character for 'he' can look a lot like that for that of 'de' when written in Senoja formal script."

"Then you're not only a monk but a student of languages, Nuvin?"

"Well, yes. I speak five languages and read… eight or so, though some of those with passing familiarity only."

Anyo raised an eyebrow. *Even as a prince, I wasn't taught so many.* "That is exceptional. Cresidethian diplomats are more studious than I realised."

"My parents were not only Femithir but teachers both curious and exacting."

"The Cresidethian houses of learning? Those I have certainly heard of."

Nuvin nodded, but before he could continue, Binya's voice drifted down from further along the hall. "I've found her."

Anyo strode to her side, Nuvin close on his heels.

Binya waited at the bust of a woman; the kindness in her gaze obvious even in stone, even after centuries. And upon the plaque, written in Nasaru letters was the name 'Misha', and the date when she won the competition.

He nearly reached out to touch the base, a smile upon his lips. *Not only did she compete here, she was champion!*

"This is a wonderful stroke of fortune." Nuvin's smile split his beard. "Did the attendant mention something about a collection of stories?"

"Best we ask," Anyo replied.

The attendant was humming when they returned, and only too happy to produce a book taken from beneath his bench. "You can purchase these if you do not wish to browse our small library, but if all you seek is a little more information on Misha, she is mentioned in the final pages."

Nuvin thanked the man and flipped through, stopping to read, and it did not take long before he looked up from the page. Anyo followed along, eyes widening at the final line.

She had been entombed in Liialle's cemetery...

"Well?" Binya was glancing between them expectantly.

"She is actually here."

"In the city?"

"Yes."

Binya slapped him on the shoulder. "Time to visit another tomb, then?"

"So it is," he replied as he handed the book back to the attendant, tension from excitement flowing into his limbs. The young man regarded them all with something between curiosity and suspicion, but offered only the suggestion that they visit before the cemetery closed.

Anyo strode from the amphitheatre with a spring to his step that was not so different to earlier in the morning.

Half a dozen men in white breastplates with coloured

gauze waited outside.

Sivelii Jarnen.

The slender soldier gestured to his troops, who raised short bows. "Something has now come to my attention, something upon which I must act – and something that will tarnish our little reunion, regrettably."

"And what is that?" Anyo asked. There was no point drawing his blade.

"A bitter offer."

Anyo waited. Binya and Nuvin had moved a little closer, but neither made any gesture that could be considered threatening.

"Accompany me to Kaarsi, Your Highness – it is not so far – and I will allow your friends to do as they please. I would even allow them to compete here, should they wish to remain in Liialle."

"I am no prince." And it was not a lie, but Jarnen's smile made it clear he knew the truth.

"Disgraced former prince, then, if you must. But you will be most useful for my purposes should you join me, alive. Less so, dead." He paused. "But know that you will save the lives of your friends if you consent."

Anyo met the sergeant's gaze. There was no hint of deceit, yet that could just as easily mean the man was a fine liar indeed. *Whatever the truth, I do not have the upper hand here.* "What guarantee can you give, should I agree?"

Binya took his arm. "Anyo, this is madness."

"Simply watch your friends leave now, you will see none here follow," Jarnen offered. "That should allay your fears, should it not?"

Again, there seemed no deceit.

Nuvin leaned closer. "I have asked the birds to watch over us, we will join the others and find you."

What choice do I have? Anyo nodded, then addressed his captor. "Let me see them leave the square."

"Certainly."

Binya's jaw was clenched. "Don't do anything stupid. You have promises to keep, Anyo."

"I mean to keep them."

Together, she and Nuvin strode from the group, and true to his word, Jarnen ordered no attack, nor did anyone follow. Of course, other soldiers could have been waiting within the streets, but Nuvin and Binya would have to deal with that possibility.

Above all, Binya had to survive so that she could sing to Misha's spectre; having her killed in a scuffle now offered no chance of that occurring at all.

He turned back to Jarnen. "For how long have you known my identity?"

"Long enough to become *very* curious about your purpose here, that much I will gladly say, Your Highness."

CHAPTER 23. – ROKURA

Rescuing so many children would make them heroes. Rokura had no doubts that even without such a fact, the surviving members of Kiteka's party would do right. After all, she had spent plenty of effort separating everyone in Bedoa's lair to make sure there would be no witnesses to her foul act.

At least, none she didn't consider expendable.

Nevertheless, watching the children being carried or escorted onto the ship helped, considering some of the remaining soldiers were even laughing and smiling with the children. Those who carried the shrouded form of Kiteka upon their shoulders however, demonstrated no cheer.

No sign of the duke, nor Edazol still. A troubling or welcome turn of events?

"Are you certain we cannot simply join them?" Asaro asked from where he crouched upon the wharf beside Rokura, shielded by shadows and crates. The building above even had a large balcony that aided their concealment.

"Yes. We are lucky they did not catch up to us, and have given up already."

"What if we sneak aboard anyway? You said we should start

in Omaila."

"I am considering the capital." It would place them within reach of Takirov by sea or overland, and certainly within reach of Nokema itself. Alternatively, the Mistress of Obsidian was surely another possibility. Had she kept her word and given Iggy a face as he so clearly deserved? "Do you have a different idea?"

"What of Senoja?"

"It is closer. And more of these ships are likely to be travelling there, but I do not believe it will be as safe for either of us."

"Could it work as another way to sneak into Nasaru?"

Such a thing would depend on who exactly manned the border. Rokura the Greyshield was Exiled, but Rokura the traveller? Such a person might be able to pass. "Possibly." He sighed. "Our choices are likely limited by what is available in this harbour, in any event."

"*Accetta oxa.*"

Viareya words from behind.

Rokura turned, and three figures stood expectantly, two with hands on the hilts of their hammers. The leader wore a white sash across her leather armour, and did not hold her weapon, but instead a small book and quill.

"I do not speak Viareya," Rokura said, first in Nasaru and then in Senoja, the words returning to him with some difficulty.

But it was enough, for comprehension was clear on her face. "You appear to be missing your ship."

Rokura hesitated. A wrong word could be costly in so many ways… "Yes."

"I see. Your party was given permission for but a short stay to complete a very specific action."

He nodded.

"It is nice to see that you are not going to bother with lies. I hope your cooperation extends to names? You may address me as Isetta."

Whether Isetta was her name or title was not important; it was clear she held a position of authority. Her features were a little hard, but she bore no cruel glint in her gaze. "I am Rokura and this is Asaro," he replied, gesturing to the lad. Asaro was glancing from face to face, tension in his posture, doubtless doing his best to read the situation based upon body-language only.

Isetta consulted her book, murmuring to herself, and then a dark eyebrow rose. "Interesting." She glanced at her men, gesturing both to take up positions on the other side of the crates… to safeguard whatever was to follow? They complied, and it did seem the two were now watching the flow of workers and visitors upon the wharf.

Asaro shifted, but Rokura gave the lad a reassuring look. An attack no longer seemed likely, and even if so, an initial struggle against one possible assailant was better than three. Instead, it appeared that Isetta was trying to ensure her next words would not be overheard.

"I believe I have an offer that you will find agreeable."

"You wish to offer us something?"

The woman nodded with a small smile as she moved closer, features clearer now. Her eyes were a striking grey. "Yes. You have a problem and I have a problem. Together, I think we might actually discover a solution."

"We are looking for a different ship, as you've no doubt guessed."

"Clearly. And I trust it is still Omaila that you wish to reach?"

"We do."

"Then I will arrange for that, but you must carry something for me, former Greyshield Rokura."

If she knew as much, what she wanted him to transport would be dangerous, in some manner. Something only a desperate Exile might take. Something she assumed a malcontent would be happy to carry… *But is that who I am?* And yet, he had committed a deep treason indeed. *To save a life.*

"If you can deliver on your promise, I would hear what you need."

"Good." Isetta's smile became a little wider. "A small object, but the message for your king will be clear. If you agree, you will be upon a ship this very evening."

Rokura glanced across the docks to the vessel Kiteka had hired, then back to Asaro, speaking a moment in Nasaru. "She is offering us passage to Omaila this night. I will need to carry something, a message to the king."

"Then I think we should accept," Asaro said, some tension leaving his body.

"It may be dangerous."

He nodded. "Doubtless. But from this point forward, everything is."

The lad had the right of it, of course. Rokura spoke now to Isetta. "Will I be permitted to know what I carry?"

"Not before I have your oath to deliver it."

Rokura shook his head, but the terms were simply far too favourable while he was in such a position of need. "Then I agree. I will carry your message to King Mutolo."

CHAPTER 24. – IGGY

Iggy clenched and unclenched his hands, linking his fingers and stretching them out. The little cracking sounds that followed were not enough to still his mind. To feel the grain of wood beneath his blade would have been better, but he could not take the time to find a suitable piece for carving, not with the sisters murmuring in their strange language, nor the poor Silent One standing nearby.

We need to leave. Mei needs me.

But the sisters did not answer.

He shook his head, letting both hands fall to his side. Mei was close, but nowhere he could simply fly through the light to – and especially not in the least because he would be blocked by whoever was supposedly able to prevent him reaching her side. The identity of such a person also lay upon his mind; someone once from Nokema?

Who?

Allowing the sisters to drag him through the night again, and thereafter relinquish control of his body, was not an option. *I'm better off using the Tonil.*

"Are you there?" It was the Silent One.

I am.

"You don't seem to be like the others. Will you hear my request?" There was a sweetness to her voice, notable beneath weariness.

To save you?

"I am a prisoner of the Sun-Killer Ascendants. They keep me hidden, only letting me free when they need me to hunt. Even now, I am not allowed to be seen, or to see others."

It hardly sounded like a life, at all. But what she asked was not possible. *I cannot take you away from this land. My goal is Kaarsi.*

"Then let me help, until I can think of something."

I trapped you easily enough – how would you help?

"I can protect you while you seek your goal. No-one can be watchful always, and no-one has limitless power, not even you. Please."

Her ability could prove useful… but that didn't actually mean she could be trusted, either.

Take them with us. They will, in fact, be extremely useful.

They? Is there another Silent One here?

No, but that is simply who they are.

Very well… but can they be trusted?

We will be watching.

Then, do you doubt their story?

Not at all. It is, sadly, a common story for Silent Ones. Rather, be wary of all – especially this close to our goal.

I am. Iggy glanced to the Tonil, which was happily munching away at one of the troughs. *How long before we reach Kaarsi? And what happens when we arrive?*

You must locate your sister and together, we await low-tide at

the Desolate Cove. There, we will confront him.

Is the Moon Father beneath the ocean?

His remaining Seal is submerged during high tide.

And together, we will… what? Drain his power? That's not something I know how to do, if that is what you need.

Leave that to us, dear.

Yes. Itula added, and somehow, it seemed as though she were nodding. Simply contain him as you have done today. With your sister's help, it should be possible. The Silent One can absorb any attacks, especially while the Moon Father is awakening and weaker. We will drain him.

A simple enough plan, but she had not described it in terms of certainty. Or much detail. *And if Mei and I cannot contain the Moon Father?*

You must. The Mistress had grown stern once more. We are all taking a risk, Iggy.

I won't force Mei to help. She can decide.

Nor would we ask you to do such a thing.

He nodded. *And the Silent One?*

The Tonil can carry you both easily. You will reach Kaarsi soon enough, with the Tonil to help.

Iggy turned back to the Silent One. *What is your name?*

"Zeana… Zee, actually."

He nodded. *Hold tight, Zee.*

CHAPTER 25. – MEI

Mei stood upon the striped shell, Thorn nearby, and closed her eyes. Would it even help, to block off her vision? It hadn't in the past. Whenever she'd called to Iggy before, imagining him first was easier without distractions all around, but when they'd been closer together, such extra steps had never been necessary.

When she steeled herself and cried out his name now, however, the power that coursed through her mind seemed that much greater – and it was already a blasting call that echoed across the lands.

Thorn was there too, his presence like a stone wall. It prevented unwanted minds from noticing her, even as they searched – through him, the sense of their probing was clear yet he rebuffed them all easily.

"Call again," he said.

Iggy, can you hear me?

Mei? A pause. *Is that really…? Mei! Where are you? Tell me, are you safe?*

It was him! She swallowed back a sob, a smile upon her face. *Iggy.*

Yes, Mei, what's happening?

I'm safe for now, what of you?

I'm safe too. I'm nearby, in Senoja – it's a long story. There was a slight doubt in his voice… was he with others? If so, it would hardly be a surprise. He would have needed help from someone at least for some of his journey, surely. *You didn't have to leave the village for me, you know.*

You're my brother.

Thank you.

Mei stiffened at an intrusion – Thorn. Like the final stretches of their ride to the City of Rope, she could no longer speak, not with her mouth or her mind.

But Thorn could.

And he used her voice. *Iggy, I don't have much time. You must come to Kaarsi, right away. We have to stop the Moon Father.*

I'm already on my way.

That's perfect. Please hurry, Iggy. Promise me. Mei ground her teeth but that was all she could do – she couldn't even step down from the Wild Shell in an attempt to possibly break the link that connected them.

After a moment of what could have been shock, Iggy answered. *I will be there –*

And then he was gone.

"We must leave," Thorn said as he pulled her from the shell. "I've sent a decoy but we cannot spend another moment here."

Mei pulled back with a glare. "What was that?"

"Necessary. We're leaving."

And then he was charging across the rooftop garden, back to the rope-ladder, across the roof and the stack of feed, and then through the courtyard. Mei kept pace, limbs fuelled by anger as much as the urgency.

The gates were still open, morning light spreading across the steel now; beyond, their carriage remained.

Once again, the guards didn't bother them and Mei found herself breathing a little sigh of relief when she slumped into the seat and closed the curtain. The horses were already moving and the rumble of the wheels and clack of hooves over stone became somewhat soothing, and she was soon blinking.

She caught herself and straightened in her seat. Ridiculous. It was no time to fall asleep. Thorn's warning should have kept her alert. Were Sun-Killers and other forces now closing in, or had his decoy worked? *I finally got to speak to Iggy too. I should be overjoyed.*

Instead, doubts continued to chip away at her mood.

Who was helping Iggy? Why had he travelled to Senoja? Was he truly safe? He seemed to be holding back something… Most galling, however, was Thorn. He'd effortlessly disrupted her plan to warn Iggy with his intrusion.

She turned to face him. "You knew, didn't you?"

"Of course. I would have been surprised had you *not* been planning to warn your brother."

Once more, the vast gap between their power – and knowledge – was made obvious. Hiding something from such a man was impossible. She could have let her shoulders slump, but instead she leant forward and clenched her hands beneath the seat. "Then I will say it aloud. I mean to escape, with Iggy. You said yourself, you need his strength, which means you can either work with us, and start being trustworthy, or you can face the Moon Father alone."

He shrugged. "A good speech, but I must call your bluff."

"I meant what I said."

"Then answer me as much. Will you turn your back on what is right? The Moon Father will come for everyone, and you and your brother are needed."

The bastard knew her answer but even so, there was no way to believe in him and so she said nothing.

Thorn waved a hand. "Having a conscience is no fault."

"That is not what bothers me. It is you," she said.

"Understandable. But I imagine your brother will feel the same about the need to protect people."

"*I* will ask him."

He nodded.

"And you might as well tell me exactly what this advantage you've mentioned is, other than Iggy himself."

"Both of you, do not forget. But put simply, the Nokema are the lost children of the Mother Sun, or Daridi, who buried herself on an island long ago. If you wish, I can tell you a shortened version of the story."

Mei narrowed her eyes at his words. "Will it help me understand what you seem to be claiming?"

"Very much so." He leant back as if to get a little more comfortable. "I will touch on the key moments. Daridi and Kaziuu had always been in competition for custodianship of the lands, eventually agreeing to split their watch in half. Kaziuu would care for the darkness, the half we call night. The Mother Sun would obviously watch over the lands the other half – day."

"That sounds like agreement."

"Yes. But a great fissure appeared in their relationship. None of my research explains what it was, but afterward, Daridi became violent and Kaziuu became duplicitous. Suffering of human, animal and nature alike was vast during the skirmishes when they encroached upon each other's domains, but in time the two discovered that after a defeat, the victor would weaken, effectively suffering an equal lessening. They were bound to each other."

"But you said Mother Sun buried herself. Why?"

He smiled. "Because she grew weary of the pointless cycle, and in doing so, forced Kaziuu into the same weakened state."

"But he is trying to break free somehow."

"Invariably."

"Then our ancestors put the seals in place?"

"A *very* long time ago, yes."

She frowned across at him. Surely, at least some traces of that story should have survived in the village? Especially when it came to the Moon Gate. "How is Daridi responding to all of this?"

"Apparently, with a refusal to return. I presume that is because she wishes to keep the Moon Father in a weakened state, and let the Guardians stand against him."

Not a wonderful turn of events for the Guardians – if any of it was true. "I hope you aren't expecting Iggy and I to help you wake Daridi."

"Not at all. But in the same way that the Moon Father's grains can act for him and store great power, there is a certain sand that can be found on the island where Mother Sun is sleeping."

"Then you mean…"

"I do. We need the cursed Black Sand of the Raging Isle."

CHAPTER 26. – ANYO

There waited a darkening camp some distance beyond the city walls, a small row of tents and a picket line, campfire cold, sentries quick to reach for weapons at their approach. Upon recognising Jarnen, the sentries stood aside.

Anyo noted the stockpiled weapons and supplies as he was led to a stump and told to sit, while Jarnen strode off to speak softly with the others. Two things struck Anyo, one of course was being left unbound and seemingly unguarded, but the second was an equally obvious fact: Jarnen and his men were still not taking lodging within the city walls.

So, what exactly are they hiding? What's their purpose?

When the Sivelii returned, it was with a flask of the incredibly dry Senoja wine. "This is a celebration, after all," he replied when Anyo asked. This time, the man spoke Senoja with a far northern accent, but Anyo followed without trouble.

"Your fortunes have changed?"

"Yes." Jarnen grinned. "With you as my bargaining chip, we can be reinstated."

"And who are 'we', exactly?"

"Officially, we have been disbanded, but once we were

known as the Black Blades."

Anyo spoke through clenched teeth. "I have heard the name." The Black Blades were known for their lack of qualms when it came to tasks the emperor would not ask other soldiers to perform; the slaughter of children not the least among them.

"Good. Then you are aware of what I am trying to rebuild – and that I will not be stopped."

"Including selling a former prince to the emperor as a spy?"

"Not so difficult to imagine. In fact, it is a lovely cloak to use. Even here in Senoja, we have heard of the so-called Beggar Prince and the life he saved. Such bitter dedication to justice…"

"It *was* the right thing to do."

"Oh, assuredly."

"You believe I sacrificed everything, my wealth, title and family, and fled my home into banishment as a ruse? So that I could in fact, eventually, spy for my father?"

He nodded. "Impressive dedication."

Anyo had to smile. After all, not so long ago, he'd faced Mei with similar suspicion, similar doubts and found himself unable to be certain of all she said. Now, the roles were reversed and he found himself aware that convincing Jarnen would be impossible. "Very well. If you have caught yourself a valuable spy, I would know – am I to be ransomed? Exchanged?"

The soldier shrugged. "That is for the emperor to decide. I must only take you to Kaarsi, arrange for a ship and await a well-earned reward."

"Perhaps your reward is the luck that you have already spent, in stumbling across me to begin with."

"I would prefer to call it tenacity, Your Highness – we spent many months scouring the borderlands for even a hint of a likely candidate, be they prince, noble, or high-ranking soldier."

Anyo shrugged. "Then tell me this, where are my friends?"

"Likely in the city – they're no use to me."

"Is that the truth?"

"I told you, they are worthless." The sergeant gestured to his men. "Get him into a tent."

After having his hands bound, then shoved and prodded into a nearby tent, Anyo lay back to glower up at the roof. Escape was tricky. What he needed was a distraction. But as the night dragged on, and the camp grew increasingly quiet, no clever ideas came to mind.

Instead, doubt crept in.

Was Jarnen lying about having no interest in everyone else?

A cry rang out.

Anyo sat upright, twisting to reach for a blade that was no longer by his side, hands still bound. *Fool.*

He crawled from the tent and there, a new light source grew.

It rested a mere dozen paces away, far too bright to be anything other than a harbinger of danger; its silvery-blue colour sent a shiver up Anyo's spine as he scrambled to his feet. More shouts of shock and concern filled the night, one man leaping over a pack as he charged toward the light.

Another sand-wraith.

One of the Senoja, his lean torso trembling in the light, stood beside the creature, staring up at the moon... yet this was far worse than what had occurred in the Black Pony inn. Luminous sand flowed from the soldier's eyes, tricking down his chest and stomach and pants, pooling not at his feet, but *beneath* them – without touching the grass.

The man hovered just above the earth.

Other soldiers were shouting ideas at one another, asking questions with no answers or calling for Jarnen, their eyes bright with fear, a shrillness to each and every sound they made.

Footsteps thundered up from behind.

A hand took Anyo's shoulder and shoved him aside. He stumbled over a tent peg, glaring up at whoever it had been – Jarnen, the man charging with blade in hand.

Bastard.

Light burst in a wave that thumped against Anyo's ears and he fell back.

A sharp hissing followed.

Screams rose, then vanished just as quickly. And all around Anyo, the hissing continued. He raised his arms, blinking hard, frantic for his vision to clear. Something hot landed upon his hands and he flinched, rolling to wipe them upon the grass.

Whatever it had been was *searing*, enough to free him from the ropes, but the grass wasn't helping much. *This isn't like the sand Binya carried.* If nothing else, the pain drove him further from the light. Still squinting, he gave more ground until he could see better.

Bodies lay spread in a circle.

A single, glowing sand-wraith waited in the centre. It was something that no longer bore the shape of the first soldier, now twice his size. Lines of sparkling sand flowed from the bodies *toward* the figure, as if feeding.

The hissing had not stopped either. It had only grown harder, and now anywhere a grain of sand lay – upon earth or blade of grass, upon the pale canvas of the tents, the barrels of water or floating through the air like tiny stars come down to visit – they sizzled.

Pain pulsed across Anyo's, blue swirling within the red of blood.

"By Aehtu!" He dashed to a water-barrel and dunked his hands, ripping them free to wipe his skin upon the nearest tent. Was it enough? Most of the blue had faded, but the taint hadn't fully disappeared from the smear of blood.

Anyo wiped harder, grunting as he ground the backs of both hands against the canvas.

A groan echoed from the sand-wraith.

His head snapped up as the sizzle of the grains grew louder still. They were moving now, swirling out from the wraith like a furious swarm of insects… *Flee, flee now!*

Anyo sprinted for the picket line. There, he found the one horse that wasn't pawing at the ground and snorting as much as the others, and snatched up a pair of saddlebags before pausing.

How close were the grains, already?

If you're going to do it, do it now! He ran back along the picket line and kicked the lead ropes free. Most horses bolted without hesitation; he only needed to smack the rumps of two, and then he was back at his chosen mount, only at that moment glancing back to the far side of the camp.

The wraith towered over the camp now, its hollow face bearing a bleeding grin of hunger.

CHAPTER 27. – ANYO

Anyo rode beneath the moonlight.

He did not drive the horse beyond safe limits but nor did he slow. He looked back at the dwindling light from Jarnen's camp every now and then, tension in his body only easing when the tree-line finally smothered the cold glow.

Even so, he could not stop – *something* drove him on.

When dawn broke, he stopped for water, stopped to feed his mount before continuing, and when the horse grew tired, he let her rest. But all the time he was pacing, all the time an urgency could not be denied.

The afternoon grew long and he found himself within a shadowed grove, slowing to a walk and leaning forward. He patted the mare's neck. "Good girl."

Anyo dismounted with a groan then, and before he had taken three steps, sunk to the loam and stretched out upon his back, his breathing growing even. *This is nice.* There was even a distant sound that was quite soothing, perhaps the crash of waves…

… and he woke to firelight and voices filled with relief.

"He's awake."

A face loomed over him, white beard and stern gaze, but a

smile upon the lips. *Han?*

Anyo rose, squinting at the firelight. Everyone was there, Katonga, Binya, Nuvin and his sisters… They all seemed well. How had such a thing happened? *Where am I, and why does my hand hurt so much?* He glanced down and a biting grain of sand remained, the skin around it chilled by blue…

"We didn't want to risk treating it," Nuvin said. "But we have an idea."

"I… what happened?" Anyo asked as he rubbed at his eyes. "Did you find Misha's tomb?" And despite his question, he nearly stood and strode to his horse, the urge to move coursing through him once more. From where did it spring? *Something is trying to hurry me along.*

"Yes. And then we followed you," Binya said with a smile. "We had a little help, and some luck, since you must have been collapsed here long enough for us to catch up."

"I escaped, after a sand-wraith attacked… wait. You found her?"

"We did. It was almost a mausoleum. Misha was well-regarded, indeed." Binya unhooked something from her belt, holding it out. "And we found this deep within her tomb, wrapped in silk that had not aged – and I'm happy to say, that it put a swift end to that wraith."

Anyo's hands trembled as he accepted a sword in its scabbard.

The sheath was plain but for a circle cut within, one that revealed the pale, luminous blade below. A persistent warmth spread from the weapon, even without drawing. The weight of centuries escaped too; that and hope, a powerful thing indeed.

He gripped the equally unassuming handle, and drew the Sothalic free slowly. Heat poured into his skin as he stared down at the object he had sought for such a long time, struggled so hard to uncover. *Rinbe, I will find a way. I'll live up to that which you and Misha guarded for so long.* Anyo blinked tears from his eyes, tasting them with his smile. *Finally, I have found you.* Or, Binya had done so – she and everyone who had helped him for each gruelling step.

"Look," Nuvin said, softly.

Faint specks of orange, red and yellow were dancing beneath the steel, as if the blade were somehow alive, a curious contrast to its pale, faintly blue colour. But that was not all, the colours had reached his hand, swirling around the wound!

Blue was fading there, rising from beneath his skin. It trickled out from his wound then, the grain from the sand-wraith winking out, carried free on the last of the blue poison.

The pain vanished.

And though the urge to keep moving had not left him, the flood of relief was welcome enough. Anyo looked up to meet the gaze of the others.

"It worked," Katonga said with a grin. "Good to know."

"Only certain targets will feel the sting of its fire," Nuvin said. "It is written that while the blade may cut down friend and foe alike, that its true power is seen against the Moon Father's children, along with the Father himself."

Anyo nodded. "Then before we find out exactly what that means, you must tell me what Misha had to say." Amongst all the relief, elation and new hope, amongst a sudden impatience to act that was not at all related to whatever was drawing him onward, there was room for disappointment.

Even jealousy.

Somehow, I always thought I'd be the one to actually find the Sothalic.

"She was beautiful and gentle," Binya said, a touch of fondness in her voice. "And she was more than happy for me to deliver the Sothalic to you, but I could not keep her very long."

"I see."

"She did ask me to pass on a message to you."

"Yes?"

"Misha said that if you're going use that blade for anything more than stopping the Moon Father, that she hopes you can become the leader Rinbe might have been."

He had no response at first. A grave responsibility, indeed. But he gripped the sword a little harder. Encouragement from the ghost of a great woman… and given without either reservation or condition.

He stood. "If everyone is rested, we should leave."

Nuvin was nodding as he reached for water to douse the fire, steam rising as he did. "We are quite close to Kaarsi as things stand. One of Daridi's Great Seals lies on the outskirts of the city, at the water's edge."

The words seemed to unlock an even greater urge to begin travelling again – and in the direction of the ocean. Was it the Sothalic? *Of course not. The urge began before I even held it.*

"Anyo, I'd like a moment." Binya had joined him as the others continued to work on breaking camp.

"Is something wrong?"

"Perhaps." She hesitated, then took a breath and gestured for them to move into the trees, somewhat. He did so and her face became shadowed. She kept her voice low. "Do you remember what you asked me?"

"About my secrets."

"Yes. I am telling you now – you might be tempted to act

against one of those deep desires tonight."

"Meaning what, Binya?"

"You want to be king."

"If I must, I will take up that burden."

She took his arm. "No, Anyo. It is something you *want*, something you believe that you deserve more than any other, and whether you can admit it now is not important. What I'm warning you against is some misguided desire to sacrifice yourself so you can save others."

"Binya…" Was she trying to manipulate him? Her words… But *someone* had to stop the Moon Father. *If it must be so, perhaps even at the cost of my life.* To save so many, was that a worthwhile price, when so much would be left undone?

Not for Binya, which was no surprise.

"You have to survive," she said.

"I will keep my word," he replied with a frown. "And if you are so worried, then I take it this means I can count on you to help protect me out there."

"That's not what you hired me for."

"Your scream did something to that first wraith, didn't it? I don't understand. Why are you…" His voice was growing louder but trailed off – the answer was obvious.

She was afraid.

Not just of losing her dreams, but it seemed Binya feared for her own life in the coming struggle. And why shouldn't she be wracked with doubts? Her anger and frustration certainly could be understood. *We're about to face something* far *beyond what any of us have faced before.* "If you are afraid, I will not be one to judge."

"I…"

He placed a hand over hers. "Listen to me. All I expect from you now is that you do what you believe is right, for yourself. I would have failed again without you, Binya. You have already lived up to your side of the bargain. Now, let me do the same."

"You noble bastard," she muttered before continuing. "This is exactly the kind of behaviour that I'm worried about, you know." Could she have been smiling?

"Just admit I'm right and let's finish this."

"Don't get used to it." She placed her free hand upon his a moment, then let go, turning back toward the campsite. "I won't ask you to promise me again, but I think I trust you, Anyo."

Finally.

He started after her, gripping the Mirror Blade tight.

CHAPTER 28. – MEI

Her second visit to the heat of the Raging Isle and its empty beach of Black Sand was achieved in but an instant.

Thorn had shown her something astounding – how to ride the sunlight, likening it to the rope and baskets of Kaarsi. Now, she was pacing the shoreline, dark grains everywhere, the sound of the waves a gentle but persistent roar, the blue horizon seemingly endless.

But at least it gave her heartbeat time to settle.

While travelling the rays, heat had surged through every bone in her body, stopped so very close to pain, and then she was stepping out onto the Raging Isle. It was just her heart that needed to catch up, or maybe her blood. A rush and thump filled her, imparting such energy that if she had wanted to, she could have set off at a sprint and circled the entire island without breaking stride once.

Or so it seemed.

Maybe my mind is getting carried away, too. But if she concentrated on the sunlight at least, countless individual beams seemed possible to climb…

"It is not that simple, Mei," Thorn said from behind her.

He had knelt in the sand, scooping large handfuls into an empty pack.

"What do you mean? That seemed easy enough, even with you guiding me. What did you hold back?"

"Nothing." He did not pause his work. "Since I can't be bothered dealing with the rippers, why don't you join me with that pack of yours so we can leave?"

Mei dumped her own empty bag and knelt, scooping the warm sand into her hands. Each grain was subtly different, of course – some speckled with grey, others bearing just a breath of purple or sometimes, tiny, tiny spots of crimson.

But overall, it was absolutely black.

It had cursed and sickened Mamalo and the others… yet holding it, there was no sense of threat.

"I told you, we won't suffer the curse."

"And you know that, not just because of the story you told about Daridi, but because you've done this before," Mei said.

He nodded. "Twice already. And I would have visited many more times but using it… doesn't quite agree with me."

She lowered her handful. "And I am different how?"

"Your affinity with sunlight is stronger than mine, that is all."

"We all draw strength from the sun."

Thorn was frowning across at her, his pale eyes full of impatience. "Keep working."

"Fine." She dug her hands into the beach and shovelled sand into her pack. "Then answer my other questions. What is difficult about travelling by sunlight?" If the man would not reveal why he had used Black Sand so infrequently, then he could share details about the rays of sun. That information would be invaluable when it came to escaping.

"There are limits. You cannot fly off to just anyone anywhere," he replied. "Only to a place you have already visited, or to the side of someone you know quite well."

Mei nodded slowly. "That's why you were so happy I'd already been here." And probably why he had taken her by horseback to Kaarsi.

"Yes. There's a little more. Only we Nokema can do this, and even then, not everyone is strong enough – they can't handle the rush of life; it actually kills them."

Mei stopped shovelling a moment. *Why am I so special? Iggy too?*

"Yes. Iggy can travel by sunlight; I assume he has already tried to find you."

"Why wouldn't he be able? Didn't you say he could?"

"I do not know. But let me warn you that even though you now understand how to travel by sun, you will not be able to find Iggy in the same manner."

She folded her arms. "Why not?"

"Because I would stop you." Thorn rose to sling the heavy-looking pack over his shoulder. "That should be enough."

"Wait. You *want* Iggy to find us."

"When I am ready, most certainly. Which, as it turns out, is quite soon."

Just what was the man up to? Did his words mean she would see Iggy soon? Mei shook her head. "Fine. Where to now, then?"

"I am visiting Omaila to put the finishing touches on something but when I return, there is something I need to teach you about light. It will be very useful when we face the Moon Father."

And hopefully another thing she could use against him. "If you're going to Nasaru, what about me?"

"Return to the inn, since someone important will be arriving soon," he said with a grin. "Just make sure you keep that Black Sand hidden inside The Guardian."

She blinked at him. Was he really letting her act on her own? And more importantly... "Iggy."

"Of course." Thorn's body was already brightening as he turned to step into one of the sunbeams, gone between one moment and the next.

An incredibly arrogant choice... or, a painfully pointed message: she was a prisoner even when he was gone. Not just because, as he had explained before, he could find her any time he cared to by using a beam of light, but he was counting on her own conscience to keep her compliant long enough to help him destroy the Moon Father.

If that is even his true goal...

But first, unless Thorn was lying again, it was time to find Iggy.

Something trembled beneath the shoreline – near enough that vibrations reached her feet. She spun. Sand spouted in a twisting line, bearing down on her. Sand-ripper! Mei leapt back. The ripper surged by, spraying shadowy grains. She shielded her eyes and lashed out with her gift.

A heavy thud followed and sand puffed up, but it did not seem she had struck the ripper, despite a new stillness.

Mei let her senses sink beneath the ground.

Not the same as seeing it precisely, but the sand-ripper was not a formless thing in her mind's eye. It crouched beneath the surface, not so far away, a mix of red and black scales, long tail and spine with sharp prongs, six legs poised to charge once again, slotted eyes turning in her direction.

But she was already reaching for the beam of sunlight that led back to Kaarsi and The Guardian, hand gripping the beam. "Too slow," she said, and pulled herself into the light.

***

Her room in The Guardian was unchanged when she stepped into it, letting the pack thud to the floorboards. The room appeared vibrant in the golden light, almost faintly aflame, and so she used the lever to change the colour of the room to become cooler.

And then found herself pacing again, sand scraping beneath her feet.

Exactly how close was Iggy?

Where do I meet him?

Voices rose from downstairs. Not in anger, but cheer, though it faded quickly enough. The sounds should have suited the moment, but too many unknowns lingered. Would Iggy arrive in time to make plans for escape? Was Thorn able to monitor them, even from Nasaru?

Light blossomed.

And from the beams stepped Iggy. He was dressed in a worn cloak of Nasaru cut, his dark hair somewhat windswept and a faint, purple glow within his tunic. But he was already leaping into her arms before she could look closer, tears blurring her vision.

She rested her chin upon his head a moment, smiling. "I was just about to get impatient."

His arms gripped her tighter. *I'm usually faster, you know.*

"I do," Mei replied, and a weight vanished, replaced by

lightness, her body seeming to exhale, something she had forgotten was possible. "You could have told me you were going, you know."

Would you have tried to stop me? He asked as he moved back, reaching out to take her hand.

"Probably."

He gave her hand a squeeze. *Then I did the right thing.*

"Fine." Mei had to laugh. "And I want to know more, but something is wrong, Ig."

We'll trade stories after. You mean the Moon Father, don't you?

"I do," she said, and she could have been surprised – but why? He could probably feel the threat. "But it's more than that. An Exile from home brought me here, and then he called you, Iggy. It wasn't me, the whole time when we spoke. I'm sorry."

Iggy shrugged. *It's more important that I'm here, isn't it? Because I think we can actually defeat the Moon Father, with or without the Exile.*

"Thorn will make sure he returns in time, I'm sure of it. He's powerful, Iggy, like you."

Not exactly, I hope.

"What do you mean?" If she let her own senses push through the relief and joy, that after so long, after so much struggle, she could finally see and speak to her brother, Mei found something unfamiliar.

Something powerful, but equally, something *limited.*

Did it have to do with the faint purple glow from before? His tunic appeared unremarkable now…

I've had help, as I'm sure you have. And we have a plan – it's mostly to let this Thorn get in over his head.

Which might work… but who was 'we' when Iggy mentioned a plan? "You're not alone in Kaarsi?"

He shook his head. *There's someone you need to meet later. Zee. But it's actually three sisters that have been the most help. They're… travelling with me. It's not easy to explain.*

"You know I'll listen."

Well, until we stop the Moon Father, they don't have bodies. They're within me.

"Within?"

He nodded.

"Oh… Is that… a little dangerous?" she asked, then raised her hands before he could answer. "I'm not saying that you don't know what you're doing, Iggy. It's just hard not to worry when you say that."

I understand. This has been an adjustment for me, too. But they can give me a face, Mei.

She straightened. If such a thing were true… what an astonishing gift! "You're sure?"

I am.

He sounded certain indeed. And yet, a little doubt lingered – after all, could not the sisters be seeking to use his power? *Like Thorn.* "And you trust them?"

Mei, you just said you believe that I know what I'm doing.

She took his hands. "I do. But I'm still going to need to know more about these sisters. And quickly. And then, tell me what you've planned."

CHAPTER 29. – NILO

If nothing else, no-one had requested healing.

Yet that was as far as their fortune stretched, since they did not pass the city gates with their stories or disguises intact. It had not, however, been the guards in their pale chainmail who refused to accept them as Fiodan healers, but an unseen figure.

Unseen, at first.

But the Sun-Killers were obviously well-practised when it came to spotting potential spies, the woman barely visible when she had leaned forward to whisper in the ear of the guards.

And now, instead of a suitably clean and warm inn, Nilo found himself sharing a rather nondescript room with his fellow captives as outside, the night wore on. Aside from the bars on the window, it wasn't so different from any other building in the city with its circular windows and above, an enormous, ghastly basket.

Something he'd been forced to endure to arrive at the prison. *I suppose I should be proud, since I didn't throw up.*

While the guards had accepted the mirror as merely what it seemed, the Sky Mirror had revealed Mei only to be *somewhere* in Kaarsi. Most likely, a rather fine inn. And that was all Nilo knew with certainty. Once again, her captor was blocking and concealing, or perhaps also taking Mei in and out of the city too often to be found.

Not that it matters from here.

He lowered the staff and its mostly-finished serpent carving with a sigh, leaning his head against the wall of their room and closing his eyes.

"There's nothing wrong with the carving, you know," Mamalo said from where he probably still leant by the window, perhaps to alleviate the limp he'd won during a short resistance to their capture. "It would have fooled everyone else."

"I suppose it may have. I'll enjoy the compliment, then."

"The robes too, if it helps. The feathers looked authentic."

Nata sighed.

Nilo opened his eyes; she lay upon the single cot, hands beneath her head. *It's time for her to make a suggestion.* "I'm still saving my strength, you two. Do we have a plan, yet?"

"Take a hostage," Nata replied. "When we're questioned. If it goes poorly."

Nilo straightened. "Surely you're not serious? And how is it going to go anything other than poorly?"

"I'm open to better suggestions. Anyone?"

Mamalo shrugged. "Looks like we're about to find out. Nilo, I hope you have some tricks up your sleeve."

He glared. "You keep saying things like that."

"Don't you?" Nata asked as she rose, rolling her shoulders a moment, then beginning to pace… which didn't amount to many steps.

Coral certainly could be used for some nasty surprises… with preparation. "Nothing that would be ready in time."

Steel clanged and then the door squeaked open to reveal what seemed to be only a short man wearing a faded blue cloak over his pale armour. *Which doesn't mean that others aren't out there watching.* A silver circlet adorned the man's head, almost lost in somewhat unkempt, blond hair. It established him as a ranking officer at minimum. He leant against the doorframe. "I cannot remember, do you all speak a civilised language?"

"We speak Nasaru, yes," Nata replied in Senoja, and her grin was decidedly unfriendly.

But the fellow only laughed. "You know, boring spies are the worst – I think I might enjoy this."

"Enjoy…" Nilo exchanged glances with the others. Who was this fellow?

The officer did not answer. "Now, please tell me why Kaarsi and not Anikaja? Do you and your king know something I do not?"

"It sounds like there is something we should now, as visitors to Kaarsi," Mamalo said. "Are you able to help us… sir?"

"None of that will be necessary. I know you are not Fiodan, remember? And you may call me Lio." His smile faded at last, and he lowered his voice. "Let me make your next decision easier. Tell me something useful and instead of having you executed, I will allow you to bribe your way out of this mess."

A moment of silence.

"How can we trust your word?" Nata eventually asked, her eyes narrowing.

Lio paused. "Surely that is obvious? Because I am making such an offer in the first place. I am taking a risk, you are taking a risk. You see I am willing to disobey my nation, allowing you to feel more comfortable in doing the same."

"Then we are here investigating possible links between one of our noblemen and the heart-leaf trade."

"I see. And who might that be?"

"Duke Bedoa."

One of his eyebrows raised. "That *is* a name I know – but you will not find him here at this time. I wonder… perhaps you are telling the truth, perhaps not. Either way, I think I will hear your offer now. Please, impress me."

"We have little –" she began, but stopped when Lio raised a finger.

Nilo stepped forward. "There is this. It is an object of great value." He handed over the Mirror of the Sky, noting both Mamalo and Nata tense up. Yet neither spoke.

The Senoja man lifted it with a slight frown. "A hand mirror?"

"Forged with Coral magic."

Lio glanced within. "Continue."

"It assists with locating people. If you speak the name of someone you know, the mirror will show you where they are."

"This mirror can do that?"

He nodded. "Try and you will see."

The man smiled, and it was almost boyish. "Very well. Elasii." And then his smile was replaced by shock – but a pleased shock.

"Do we have a deal, then?" Nata asked.

He did not glance up from the mirror as he stepped aside, waving a hand. "That we do, strangers. Be on your way, this night. No-one will interfere with you and your most… sensitive cargo."

Nilo collected his staff and his pack and hurried from the room, Nata and Mamalo close behind.

He led them along a quiet, darkened corridor then, through another heavy door that was already open and into an entryway where more barred windows let soft moonlight inside. It fell upon a single guard at his desk. The man stood and lifted a steel bar from the doors, gesturing for them to leave.

Outside, their horses waited beside Mamalo's wagon. "What is this?" Nilo hissed as they strode from the prison.

"Don't question it," Mamalo said as he kept pace, wincing with every other step.

But no-one stopped them from mounting up or riding through the dim streets… not even as they passed a small squad of soldiers near a night market, where light and music waited. *Word from Lio travels quickly.*

And then, when they at last left Kaarsi and stopped upon the moon-lit highway, Nilo let his shoulders sag a little. Escape, but at what cost? He glanced around. No-one else upon the road, but a faint blue glow seemed to lurk beyond the nearby woods.

"I can't decide whether that was brilliant or imbecilic," Nata said where she sat astride her horse, staring back at the city.

"I can," Nilo replied. Was the blue glow actually growing stronger? "We're alive."

Mamalo chuckled. "So we are. I don't know what that man will do with such a gift, but Mei *is* in Kaarsi somewhere. We just need to sneak back inside and continue the search."

"And hide your cargo," Nilo added. "He knew and still let us go."

"True," Mamalo said with a frown upon his face. "But we have to go back inside."

"Tomorrow, at the earliest," Nata said.

"I think we might need to check something else first." Nilo pointed to the sky, which had definitely grown brighter. "Do you both see that?"

Two slow nods followed.

"Right you are, Nilo." Mamalo snapped the reins once more. "Not sure I have the strength for another surprise, but that probably won't be up to me."

CHAPTER 30. – THORN

He could not read the siblings where they sat across from him in the carriage.

A troubling turn of events.

Not enough to derail his plans, but a niggling annoyance nevertheless. At first, finding them had been the problem, then collecting one, then drawing the other close – keeping them apart for just long enough to finish preparing, to prevent them from developing any means to interfere. Now, at long last, their power could be put to use.

But *something* about Iggy was unexpected.

His strength is greater than I anticipated. Almost as if it reaches out to me. But any attempt to follow the ghostly traces that ran across his mind came to naught. The young man's power should have been a relief, but coupled with the inability to truly read the two now that they were together…

Still, the siblings would serve their purpose.

And for all their might, they were so young, so very inexperienced. The world was as much a mystery to them as their very own gifts. *There is nothing that can compare with knowledge.*

If nothing else, a little surprise remained nestled up his

sleeve – just in case.

Unlikely as it would prove to be. Ascendance was within his grasp now.

So, so close.

"Do you have to tap your foot that way?" Mei asked.

Thorn stopped with a smile. "Surely you can forgive some impatience? The time directly before momentous events is always tedious."

How close is Kaziuu to breaking free? Iggy's voice was quite calm.

"Worry not. We will reach the cove in time."

You can sense the sand-wraiths.

"A significant number, isn't it?"

Iggy leant forward, his featureless face nevertheless evoking some annoyance. *What I cannot sense, is how close the others are. It's hard to see beyond the Moon Father.*

"Which is why we need to strike him down before he is fully awoken," Thorn replied. No better time to take the mantle of a half-slumbering god, either. "And as for the Beggar Prince of Nasaru and the Sothalic, it is very near."

Mei lifted her own minor blade. "What about the third one?"

"Slinking ever-closer," he replied, now with a sigh. "Believe me, children. I have planned this night for *decades*. All the pieces have come together, either through time, chance or for the most part, by my design." Though the part about the second minor blade of Nokema was not wholly accurate, considering the true distance between the thief and the Desolate Cove.

Again, a detail that could be overlooked.

A cry of shock echoed from above and the carriage slowed to a halt.

"Just one moment." Thorn stepped out into the warm night. His feet crunched over gravel beside the road as he approached the driver. The fellow upon the stage, reins curled at his feet, stared down to the cove.

Luminous shapes stood in scores… more, even.

Their bodies were a mix of human-like and *very* human with torn clothing and fully formed hands and faces. Some had obviously been called from surrounding villages; new children to serve the Father.

It's taken a little longer than I expected.

But such a thing remained an exceptionally good sign, if Kaziuu had called so many so soon, he did *not* want to be interrupted. "Not a desire I plan to fulfil, sadly for you."

"I knew it." The driver was shuddering. "Everyone said this place was haunted."

"Feel free to return to the city," Thorn said.

He blinked down. "My Lord, will you be safe?"

Thorn nodded. "I will, indeed."

Footsteps approached; Mei and Iggy joining him, the young man with his hood raised, face shadowed in the night.

Mei's jaw was set as she glared down at the wraiths. "What now?"

"Do you remember what I taught you? Channel to me, and together we can overcome."

Both nodded but Iggy had folded his arms. *It's hard to believe we will be enough to destroy a god, even one that is only waking.*

"Daridi keeps him reduced, remember?"

Still. We're taking an unfathomable risk for you.

Thorn spread his hands. "Then let me say, not only that we three are the strongest from Nokema in generations, but there is something else in our favour – not just the Mirrors of Sothalic."

Mei's hand shifted to the weapon at her belt. "What else have you been holding back?"

"The sun, remember?"

She frowned and Iggy shook his head. *Did you really keep enough Black Sand for that?*

Thorn chuckled. "Of course. I didn't use it all back in Omaila. Or at the inn, if that is your concern. The leylines are open now, the Tree focuses such power across the nations to me and we are together at last, yes. But even so, there's still something for Mei to do with what I saved."

"I remember what you taught me," she said. "I just don't believe *you* actually think I'll be able to recreate the sun."

"We are none of us so grand," Thorn said. *At least, not yet.* But soon enough, such things would not be out of reach. "Enough of Daridi lingers within the sand that you can cast a tiny sun into the air, weaken Kaziuu and destroy his children. The prince and others will protect you while you do so. Iggy, you will assist me directly, at first."

Iggy seemed to hesitate.

Mei put a hand on his shoulder. "I can do this."

All right.

"But we have one more question, Thorn."

He stared down to the shore, where the last of the seal would have darkened by now – he'd made sure of that, but there was time to humour them a little longer. "Yes?"

"When were you Banished? Who are you?"

"Two questions, then." Not surprising ones, but his answer would likely disappoint them. "Long before you were born, and thus my old name would mean nothing to either of you."

He could be lying but we'll never know, Mei. Iggy shrugged. *He's obviously been interested in us for a long time.*

The clack of approaching hooves reached Thorn from beyond the nearest bend in the road. "That will be Anyo and his friends, at last." He clapped his hands together. "Please take a moment to explain before joining us, Mei."

Then he gestured for Iggy to follow, and started down toward the Moon Father – and toward to a destiny so unlikely that it could have been just another lie heaped upon the others.

And yet, it was not.

To Ibila, he sent only one thought. *Soon, I will not have to spend even another moment away from you.*

CHAPTER 31. – ANYO

Anyo slowed his mount, raising a hand for caution.

Ahead, an ornate carriage waited by a trail leading down to the ocean. Who had reached the cove first? But the light drew his attention. A mighty arch of stone presided over what appeared as nothing more than a field of sand-wraiths; their glow powerful enough to light the place so that the height difference between two figures approaching was stark.

Even with the Sothalic, how can I defeat so many?

The others had slowed too, their own silence a clear indication of doubt.

"Anyo."

He turned. A young woman approached from the carriage, her bearing familiar. And when she reached him, her serious expression, her pale skin, blonde hair… "Mei of Nokema?"

"Yes." She did not seem at all surprised to see him. "We don't have a lot of time. That man down there with my brother is trying to replace the Moon Father. We need your help to stop him, and then the awakening god." She raised a long dagger with a pale blade, hints of fire within. "As it so happens, I have a minor blade, sister to your Sothalic, but I need someone to wield this while I work on something else."

Anyo found himself staring, mouth open.

Not only did she speak near-perfect Nasaru now, not only did she carry something like the Sothalic, but she was also aware of *and* trying to stop the Moon Father…

Nuvin spoke in Anyo's place. "Young lady, you are a Guardian, I presume?"

"I suppose I am. Will you help us?"

"We will," Anyo said, finally finding his voice. "Are you certain you can use your power to face them?"

She smiled. "I'm a little stronger than when we last met."

He would have to take her word for it. "Very well, what do we do?"

"Keep the wraiths off me while I create a tiny sun with this." She lifted a handful of what appeared to be black sand from a pouch… difficult to tell in the moonlight, but it put him in the mind of whatever had powered the Sky Carriage.

"A tiny sun… Perhaps you can, at that. So be it." Anyo glanced over his shoulder. "Han?"

"Aye, lad." Han accepted the dagger from Mei.

"Everyone else remember – don't let them touch you. Any wounds, let me or Han purge you after."

Nods from those gathered, and he paused at Binya. Her jaw was clenched but she had not turned back. "You know we won't be much help down there, Anyo."

"Just be my eyes if they surround me."

"We will."

Mei was already moving.

He drew the Sothalic and started down the slope after her, drawing closer to the mass of sand-wraiths and the two figures before them. The shorter one was obviously Iggy, but the second was familiar, even from behind. Something about the way the man held himself, even his clothing…

Anyo lowered the legendary blade.

Father?

What was the king doing, standing on Kaarsi's windswept beach and, according to Mei, trying to assume the mantle of the Moon Father? *That makes no sense. None at all! Mutolo is no Sorcerer, in any event…*

Inspiration struck.

Unless, could that have been what the Coral Tree was for? Setting the issue of accuracy regarding his wild guess aside, the king simply could not have been down there. *Is it truly him?*

Mei turned back. "We have to hurry."

"That is the king."

She frowned. "What?"

"The man standing beside your brother is King Mutolo, my father."

Mei turned back, and immediately shook her head. "That is Thorn. A Nokema Exile. Anyo, we don't have time for this."

And she was right, for something large was stirring below, trying to push itself up from beneath the very sand.

But still, he caught Mei's shoulder. "Please. Tell me what you see. Describe him."

"A man from my village. Tall, grey hair and dark stubble. He's wearing the armour of a Senoja." She stopped listing things at his expression, which must have reflected the chill he felt at hearing her matter-of-fact description, with not a shred of hesitation.

Then… the reason he changed all those years ago… the man was an imposter?

For no matter what she said, it appeared that a slightly older but still very upright man from the royal Nasaru family stood upon the beach, familiar face clean-shaven.

"I see what Mei has described," Nuvin said softly.

Han muttered a curse. "I see the king."

"Anyo, I'm sorry that you've been deceived – we all have," Mei said. "Please, I need your blade. I need the man who captured me in the marsh and who would not give up on his quest, no matter the set-back."

His knuckles whitened around the hilt. "Of course."

And now she set off down the trail at a run. He followed to where she planted her feet in the sand, not so far from the line of luminous wraiths. Anyo stood before her, glancing over his shoulder. She was jamming the black sand into a ball in her hands, adding something wet from a bowl, then closing her eyes to focus her power, it seemed, as a warm light began to glow.

"Anyo, look!" Nuvin called.

The sand wraiths moved, flowing forward. And though Iggy and… Thorn stood closer, the creatures were driven around the pair by some unseen force.

Han appeared beside him, small mirror blade in hand. "We buy her whatever time she needs."

"We do." He raised his voice. "No-one stare into their eyes!"

Together they leapt forward.

The first creature reached him, unfinished arms stretching; he focused on them, not the thin face, and swung the Sothalic. Invisible flames crackled. Pale steel hit with a hiss and the creature collapsed into a pile of sand, the blue and silver light vanishing like smoke.

So effortless!

He spun to slash through another, and then a third. Each time, the blade reduced them to nothing, banishing their light and power. Despite their vast numbers, the wraiths seemed to narrow their path, aiming for he and Han alone – equally pleasing and troubling.

Anyo ducked and swung up with both hands, cutting through two wraiths at once. Beside him, Han too, seemed to be experiencing just as much success.

"They're trying to flank you!" Binya called.

Anyo gave ground and found one of the more fully-formed wraiths circling. Unlike the others, it seemed far more human. Did that make it more intelligent or purposeful than the others? It bore defined limbs and even wore a simple, mostly intact tunic, and had features that were recognisable as a face.

A face with a strained smile, a nose and eyes –

Don't look. Anyo charged after and swung from the side, slicing the thing into naught but a pile of sand.

Binya and the others had formed their own small wall before Mei, whose ball of light was growing.

A curse echoed across the beach.

Wraiths swarmed over Han. They pulled him to the ground as his mirror blade continued to cut deep. Anyo roared as he leapt after. He skewered a trio of the wraiths but their numbers bore down on him too, dragging at his shoulders, cold searing through his body.

But he clung to the Sothalic's warmth, swinging at the wraiths as he reached for Han amongst the hail of sand.

Golden light blazed overhead.

Pain vanished.

Every single wraith collapsed in a single thud of sand that echoed across the cove.

And the light only grew brighter, rays pouring down in such a sparkling array that he had to shield his eyes. "Han?"

"I'm alive."

Relief flooded his limbs but it was short-lived.

Something *ancient* was rising from the sand, somehow holding shadows around itself as it broke free. Unbelievable power spread from its indistinct form, such that Anyo gasped for air.

The beach was darkening, even with Mei's sun.

He fell to one knee but managed to raise the Sothalic. *If I can just hurl it at the Moon Father, maybe…* The warmth within the blade was not fading but his arm trembled. He could not find the strength.

Anyo hit the sand with a groan.

He craned his neck as his vision failed, and there, beneath the light, Iggy and the shape of his father had not crumbled.

CHAPTER 32. – MEI

The others had collapsed around her. Further along the beach, Anyo and Han had fallen too, but Mei stood firm despite the Moon Father's monstrous power.

It was easily enough to dim the light from her sun, which would likely soon be extinguished as Kaziuu continued to take shape. All around him now, grains of silver sand were lifting. More wraiths? It could have been an army, one so, so immeasurable – unstoppable – but instead, the glowing grains drifted up to form a latticed dome of stars.

Enough to light the otherwise darkened shoreline significantly; it could have been day, although a day of silvery blue. The dome also imposed a hush upon the beach, so that the soft crash of waves receded.

In the centre of it all, his form now clear, many arms raised, the Moon Father towered over Thorn.

The creature had changed somewhat from her vision at the seal.

Silver now streamed from his wide mouth, face an uncanny mix of decaying tortoise and human, but with bat-like ears atop. Glimmering sand poured from the ears and empty eye-sockets alike, his skull seeming so full that no eyes could move within. The same steady eruptions appeared on the body, coating folds of blackened skin, as if to rejuvenate. Even the Moon Father's six hulking arms and legs bled at the joints.

But unlike the wraiths, the Moon Father did not trail sand as he moved.

The luminous grains clung to and were absorbed by his body, only to pour forth once again in a seemingly endless cycle.

And from his living-corpse exuded more and more of the power Mei had not at first noticed, and was almost squeezing her very limbs together. She stumbled forward, drawing nearer to Iggy.

The force of an awakening god – thunderous might, even in a weakened state. It drove her to one knee. *We're not threats. We're invisible to such a creature.*

But Thorn did not falter where he stood, blood smeared across his cheek.

Nor did Iggy.

So, too, a new figure that approached, crossing the sand slowly but steadily enough. It was Zeana arriving, the Silent One, as arranged. And despite the way red wrappings upon their head evoked a helpless look, or the way their shoulders trembled, they did not fall.

Could the Silent One make a difference?

There hadn't been time for Iggy to explain everything – only that Zee would help distract Thorn, since Thorn assumed he had an ally in Zeana. *Iggy and the sisters are certain enough.* The bigger concern was whether Thorn could stop the Moon Father. Even with the link he had forged between herself and Iggy?

No need to despair, Mei. Thorn's voice rang in her mind – bright with anticipated victory, it seemed. Yet his confidence did not instil itself within her. *We are slowing him. This is exactly the chance I have been waiting for – you mustn't forget your part.*

She looked to her brother. *Iggy.*

We can do this, Mei.

How? He's going to betray us, even if we do stop that thing.

Iggy had clenched both hands. *We have to trust each other.*

I know. But when she finally drove herself upright, reaching for what remained of the Black Sand, she had none of the Coral extract Thorn had provided.

Any moisture is better than nothing to begin the binding. Impatience filled Thorn's voice now.

Mei glanced to the sea… too far, surely. *Think!*

And then the simplest answer came to her.

She stuffed the Black Sand into her mouth. Grit stung her tongue, caught between her teeth as she chewed. Yet heat and strength flowed free, setting her limbs to twitching but not enough to make her stop. *I have to do this.*

Mei spat the ball into her palm, and pulled in what light she could. Though it blazed in gold, the size was so much smaller. It wouldn't be enough.

Good, Mei. Thorn's voice in her mind suggested a nod, but he had not turned from the Moon Father, body rigid with effort. Kaziuu's own arms were now raised, hands shaped like claws. *Do not stop there, Mei – gather all the light you can.*

She tried to draw more from within the sand, more from somewhere within herself, as though taking what she had stored over the previous day – and it worked! Her breathing grew ragged but the ball of light brightened.

Cast the second sun, Mei, Thorn instructed. *We will handle the rest. Iggy, you need but lend me your strength.*

I will take what I need from him. Iggy's reply was firm.

Of course.

But Mei did not release her light right away. Was it enough? Foolishly, she glanced around, perhaps for one last piece of advice; from who, she did not know, but everyone was lying motionless upon the sand still. They seemed alive, but for how much longer?

In her hands, the golden light had not dimmed. But there was no more Black Sand, this was the final chance. *Surely, I need more than this? We're facing a god, after all!*

She hadn't asked anyone in particular, not really.

And it did not seem an answer would come, not with the Moon Father looming above. Not even Iggy seemed able to take his attention from –

No. I can't give in to doubt. Iggy had risked and suffered so much just to stand upon the beach before the Moon Father, to not only win a face, and a proper life for himself, but so that he could protect others.

And he expected her to live up to the promises she made. *He trusts me.*

"And I trust you, Iggy."

This time, Iggy would be the one doing the protecting but she still had a part to play. She owed him and everyone else who depended on her actions now, to act. Not to be frozen by doubt.

Mei forced more of her own light into the ball of Black Sand, gripping it hard as she could, heat spreading through her hands and rushing up to her elbows, as if she could squeeze the light down into something sharper and brighter, something more powerful – something not only born of the Mother of Sunlight, but her own defiance.

The tiny sun crackled.

Mei hurled it into the air. It flew toward the dome's roof and hung there, rays searing down upon the Moon Father now.

Silver spluttered as his slow face twisted up.

Thorn ripped his arms in a downward motion.

A strip of flesh peeled from the Moon Father in response. Dark and glittering, it rolled free and struck the beach with a muted hiss. New skin of a pale blue was revealed – this time smooth, beautiful even.

But the Moon Father howled; a scream that could not be heard but which still whipped up sand and wind. Mei shielded her face, only for the gust to die away quickly. Thorn was already clawing at the air again, and in response, another strip of flesh was torn free. The Moon Father reached out now, ungainly but with purpose.

Stop him. Thorn's voice rang out.

Iggy twisted his torso and a wave of invisible power burst from him, leaving his entire body trembling. But it was enough! The Moon Father was slowing, his many sharp fingers unable to reach down to Thorn.

The false king of Nasaru did not seem to be taking his chance for granted.

His arms were a blur now, and the slices of power that cut with each movement all the same; but Mei could barely follow each with her mind. Yet if the man's plan to defeat the Moon Father meant flaying the enormous figure down to some smooth, clean, under-skin, then it was working.

Strips of blackened flesh flew through the air like ebony ribbons, silver spraying with them. Nothing fell close enough to strike Mei, but she still took a step back, heel sinking into soft sand.

A vast pressure within the dome was growing again; the Moon Father fighting back?

Scraps of old flesh remained upon the hands and in joints, and for the most part Kaziuu was now an incandescent being perhaps more impressively god-like. Luminous sand continued to flow from the ancient face, mouth moving, chewing the silver as it spoke or roared or something... but all without sound.

Not even with her mind could she discern whether it was trying to communicate or curse.

Now, see my ascension, siblings of Nokema.

Thorn plunged a fist into the bag of Black Sand at his waist. When he drew it forth, the cursed sand burned orange in his fist. He glanced over his shoulder, a hunger reflected in his eyes. "Ready?" He spun and flung it at the Moon Father.

Grains shot forth in a streak that trailed sparks – and tore the god's head clean from its shoulders.

CHAPTER 33. – MEI

Before Mei could finish her gasp, Thorn had leapt after the Moon Father.

The enormous torso was tumbling. It struck the sand with a boom that shattered every star in the dome. Waves crashed in after, reaching the tips of Kaziuu's hands and there, the water sizzled into steam.

Thorn had not slowed.

He was already bent over the Moon Father's neck, gorging himself on the silver that flowed, hands a blur as he crammed mouthful after mouthful into his face. Plenty spilled down his shirt as he swallowed, eyes like twin points of flame.

Of greed.

Mei charged, swinging her own arms.

The tiny sun she'd created plummeted. It struck Thorn in a shower of blinding light… and when her vision cleared, he was still eating.

She faltered.

A hand came to rest on her shoulder. *Just get him talking, Mei.*

Iggy stood beside her, and she knew from his voice, he was smiling. He hadn't given up. The sisters were yet to play their hand; it was no time to give up. Mei crossed the sand to stop before the Moon Father's corpse. The smooth blue was sinking into the sand now, as though all the silver draining from within was shrinking it – or stealing its solidity.

Thorn had not stopped eating; up to his elbows in the blood of a god now.

How to get him talking?

There were no words she could use that would appeal to any compassion or shame; Thorn obviously carried neither. She could not threaten or fool him either. He'd been so many steps ahead the entire time she'd been his captive and even now, the link between them lingered.

Could he read her thoughts still?

He had not seemed to during the struggle with Kaziuu. And so all that remained was… bargaining? *Will he believe that I'm desperate enough to sink that low?*

"Thorn. I want to change the terms of our deal."

He did not stop eating, but he did face her now. "Do you?"

"You can grant us what we've fought for."

"So I can," he replied between mouthfuls, giving a shrug. "But you can grant me nothing – you have already served precisely your purpose, Mei."

She frowned. "Then help because no-one else is powerful enough!" Flattery. Clumsily disguised as anger, but doubt probably lent her words some emotion, if nothing else.

Thorn chuckled through his ghastly meal.

Mei.

She stepped aside as Iggy joined her. His own hands were covered in silver, but when he pointed them at Thorn, glints of purple, pink and crimson swirled *into* his skin, vanishing already. *Like the way he drinks.*

As before, Iggy's limbs were trembling as he readied his gift – it radiated from him in waves that were both stronger and different to anything he'd summoned before. Mei had to shield herself, even though the power was… calmer than what had borne down from the Moon Father, who'd been unfinished.

Which meant, he was receiving assistance from the Sisters at last. Why had they chosen now to help; was Thorn somehow more vulnerable? The Sisters had never really explained the details of their plan, but Iggy had asked her to trust them, and she trusted her brother.

Ready yourself, fledgling god. Iggy's voice rang out in her mind.

Thorn swallowed, taking a moment to lick his lips before spreading his arms wide. "As you wish."

Was it confidence from his own power, or did Thorn have yet another trick up his sleeve? Did he even need another surprise at this point? He had already devoured so much.

A glimpse of red caught her eye, rising from behind the massive corpse.

Zeana, the Silent One.

Was Zee actually *Thorn's* final gambit? Had the Silent One betrayed them? Did Iggy know?

"Iggy, wait!"

But a blast of psychic energy roared across the beach. Sand, silver and fragments of blackened skin alike flew through the air as the Silent One leapt before Thorn.

Her brother's attack struck with a mighty thunderclap – and shot back.

Too fast.

Iggy would never be able… a second concussion shattered the night air, tossing Mei to the ground. She pushed herself back up, ears ringing, and her brother stood calm and composed.

Somehow, unharmed.

How?

Thorn lay slumped across the Moon Father's corpse, unmoving. Zee was crawling away, shuddering with each movement, but they had obviously fared far better than Thorn, not having been Iggy's target.

Mei glanced back to Iggy. *Did you… reflect the reflection?*

He nodded.

Did you know that you could do that?

It's something the sisters and I planned. I didn't tell you everything, in case Thorn read your mind.

A wise choice.

Thorn had been manipulating Zee from a long time before we met, and he assumed I'd never notice. Iggy started toward Thorn. *Come on, we have to be sure.*

Mei hauled herself after, picking her way through the wreckage of the Moon Father to where Thorn lay face-down. Iggy kicked the man onto his back, revealing a silver-streaked face and eyes that barely flickered open. All Thorn's power seemed to have vanished; his own and whatever he'd stolen from Kaziuu.

But his eyes saw *something* when he looked up. "You are real… after all. I had… discounted you."

They are real. Iggy was the one who'd folded his arms now.

"Judge me… if you must." Thorn's words were growing softer. *No-one else came close to what I achieved.*

Mei frowned down at the man. What had he achieved but

ruin? For himself and for who knew how many others? From the moment he was banished from Nokema, perhaps. And now, he was finally receiving… some form of justice.

If Ibila asks…

Thorn grew still and the silver began to spread, even as his face changed – growing brittle, and slowly collapsing into itself. The rest of his body swiftly followed in kind.

"Is that the end of him, then? Of both of them?"

The Sisters confirm it.

She took him by the shoulders. "Did they get what they needed to help you?"

He nodded.

Mei let a shuddering sigh escape, even as she smiled. After so long! He wouldn't have to hide himself away now – he was finally going to be free.

Wait. Mei, it's not that simple. The others. Iggy took her hands and gave them a squeeze. *I have a choice to make.*

Zee lay nearby, breathing hard. And more; Mei looked back along the beach where the prone shapes of Anyo, Han, Katonga, and the others he had travelled with waited – all drawn into a struggle they ought not to have had to face. And none of them moving, none rising as if from sleep or unconsciousness.

"Are you saying…"

I am. If I ask the Sisters to save everyone, I cannot have my wish.

CHAPTER 34. – ANYO

Anyo woke to a beach that was entirely different to the one he stood upon before the Moon Father's arrival overwhelmed everyone. Instead of a glittering night, the sun was rising orange over the sea, the waves were gentle and the sand was no longer restless.

Instead of a maniacal liar who had likely long ago replaced his father, instead of a disturbing creature tearing itself free from the beach, there was a mound of sand, smooth contours suggesting the remains were buried beneath.

And unlike before, Mei stood before him with a smile of relief upon her face.

And yet, did the smile actually reach her eyes? "You're the second one to recover," she told him.

Anyo glanced around – Han, Katonga and Nuvin and his sisters, and the others who had come together for the same purpose, but no sign of Binya. Where had she gone? *She has to have survived.*

"They'll wake too," Mei said.

"Where is Binya?"

"She asked you to wait for her. She was walking along the

beach, which is pretty impressive considering what you went through."

"Why is she doing that?"

Mei extended a hand. "She didn't say."

Anyo accepted her help. Something slid to the sand as he rose; a blade as pale as white fire. Sothalic. He lifted it and if nothing else, a little thrill of triumph remained. While it and its rather surprising sibling-blades hadn't actually stopped Kaziuu, they had certainly cleared a path around the real heroes of the night. "Then you and your brother defeated the Moon Father? And the pretender?"

"We did."

"Then the kingdom of Nasaru – all kingdoms, really – owe you both a great debt," he said, turning to survey the beach, before focusing on Mei once more. "One that I will do what I can to fulfil. Should you have need of anything, simply ask. You, or your brother, wherever he may be."

"Thank you, Your Highness. I will take your offer to heart," she replied, then paused. "Iggy appreciates your offer, too. He said he hopes you will soon be able to deliver on that promise."

Anyo raised an eyebrow. "Is that a slight rebuke?"

"No, he is sincere."

"Well, he is not wrong. I have made that promise, and I will keep it. But in my father's… absence, there will be others who expect to take on his role."

Mei looked to the mound where the imposter had last stood. "Last night must have been awful."

"It was," Anyo said. And how to make sense of it? Father had been an unkind man and not always a fair ruler, but who had been responsible for which ills, and for how long? "I might tell myself now that there were signs, for many years. That I recognised them for what they were, but that would be a lie. He seemed himself enough – distant, driven. Cruel at times. Obsessed with other concerns. This is for the best."

"I hope so, for your sake, Anyo," she said. "I doubt there will be many easy days ahead now."

"There won't be. And thank you, but what of you and your brother?"

"He has gone for now. I'm joining him soon," she replied.

A little vague, but why press her? "Before you do, will you tell me what happened? By some wonder, we are alive and I suspect I ought not to be, considering what we faced here."

She nodded. "Once everyone has risen."

***

Silence filled the beach after Mei finished speaking. She sat with her arms wrapped around her knees, which she'd drawn up to her chest as she told the tale.

Of all who were gathered, only Nuvin stood afterward, pacing slowly across the sand, mouth moving with silent words spoken to himself. Everyone else sat, in part due to a lack of strength – no surprise, considering how close to death they had come.

And the silence was a reflective one rather than that of disbelief.

Anyo did not blame them.

Mei's description of the final struggle was no tall tale, perhaps not compared to the existence of the Three Fates, mysterious sisters who had lent their power, yet by the sombre expressions before Anyo, it was Iggy upon everyone's mind.

Iggy who had saved the lands, who had saved everyone

sitting upon the sand, and done so at the cost of his own dream.

"How can we repay such a sacrifice?" Katonga asked softly.

Mei stood. "Maybe just by living your lives." Light was gathering around her… or was it, in fact, that she was *becoming* light? "I haven't thanked you yet, but you all made a difference."

And then she reached up and somehow, slid into one of the bright rays.

Once more, silence settled across the beach, this time touched with a little awe.

***

Anyo found himself at least somewhat involved in the division of paths that followed – Nuvin, Elin and Fiana would return home to carry news of the success, and Mei's minor blade too, with promises to visit the capital soon.

"Upon our return, I hope to be taking audience with the new king," Nuvin had said with a smile, his sisters nodding in agreement before setting off with assurances that they would have no trouble departing from the port.

Binya appeared much consumed by something and mentioned only her obligations when Anyo asked, but he did not press her.

"Ready, lad?" Han asked. There was a little cheer in his manner as he stood beside Katonga, tapping one foot. But there was pain too and in the morning light, did the whites of Han's eyes bear a blue tint?

No, just my imagination.

"I am," Anyo said as he hefted the Sothalic. "And soon, a new king will sit upon the throne, for better or worse."

"For better, I suspect," Kat replied with a smile.

Binya nodded. "And me."

"That might depend upon Ebatru." And even though their words were welcome, doubt was stronger. *Chiotta, too. She's been moving her pieces for some time, now.*

"Then don't waste this chance," Han said.

"I won't – and I'll need your help." He linked his hands, stretching up over his head as he sighed. "Either way, we have a long road ahead of us."

EPILOGUE CHAPTERS

CHAPTER 35. – ANYO

Omaila had waited for him.

Eagerly, this time – even staying awake and alight, late into the night.

And riding the streets toward the palace, glimmering Sothalic held aloft, there had been a certain unreality about the scenes of smiling faces, torches, lamplight and cheers where they lingered in his memory. Yet the people had been thrilled to see him. Actually thrilled! The Beggar Prince, a sudden hero.

And for what? *I have not changed their lives at all.*

He crossed the darkened room to slump into an armchair of a deep, dark green, fabric cool against his forearms as he waited. Arranged near the window, he was able to reach out with one foot to part the tall curtains, just enough to let moonlight within.

It could have been hope that gave the people cheer.

But whatever promises they believed he would keep, not a single one of them would come true by itself. Someone had to put in the work. "And that someone is me. Not the others."

Balo was still somewhere in the eastern islands. It seemed

news of Father's death might not have reached him. *Father's second death, I suppose.* Ebatru had failed to appear so far, though he must have known and all rumours of his activities suggested he did. And if the returning Greyshield that Anyo was to meet this evening – only his third night in the palace since returning from Kaarsi – was correct, then nor would dear, eldest sister Kiteka.

Chiotta had agreed to a meeting upon the morrow, and so far, the palace staff had either welcomed or at least accepted his return. Father's allies, too, for the most part, though a few in particular would need to be watched.

Most would have been waiting, biding their time.

But for all Anyo's strides toward his goal, the inability to find Binya was a weight upon his shoulders. Why? Upon reaching the city, she left them to meet the obligations she had mentioned, which was perhaps no surprise. And nothing during the long trip home suggested she planned to vanish…

On one hand, not much time had passed.

On the other, Binya had been relentlessly clear about her terms of repayment. That she would delay seeking an immediate start on her demands seemed out of character, with or without her existing commitments.

At a knock upon the door, he straightened. "Yes?"

"Your Highness, if I could have a moment of your time?"

A woman.

Her was voice an unfamiliar one – cultured enough to suggest nobility, but of the few who had requested an audience, all were arranged via Katonga's precise attention to detail. Anyo smiled. It had almost been a surprise, to see the man so efficiently organise the meetings along with other day-to-day aspects of palace life.

"Who calls?"

Her voice grew somewhat softer. "My name is Ibila and I was your father's mistress."

Anyo rose, crossing the room at speed. He brightened one of the lamps, drawing attention to his weary expression in a nearby mirror, then opened the door.

She carried a lamp of her own. Ibila was an alluring woman not so old as his father had been, nor a young woman either. The mistress was dressed in red silks beneath a black robe.

"Join me," he said, gesturing for her to enter.

She did so, setting her lamp upon one of the polished sideboards. The woman calling herself Ibila moved to the curtains next, drawing them to block the last of the moonlight. "I have not heard your father speak to me in days now."

"Heard?" The statement was not at all what he'd expected. But then, Thorn had been capable of maintaining a very, very sophisticated illusion over many years. It was entirely possible the woman had never truly heard his father speak.

"Yes." She sat, and her dark eyes were troubled. "We can communicate via our minds — and it seemed he tried to reach me, weeks ago now. I want to know what happened."

"He… died in pursuit of something beyond even his ability." It was an honest answer, after a fashion. He held back his own bitterness and relief, of course. There was no need to trouble a grieving widow, for want of another word. Especially, perhaps, a widow who had been duped. *Or so I imagine…*

Ibila shook her head. "That much I could tell just from knowing him."

"I did not see his final moments. But it took many of us to

defeat the powerful evil he sought on the beaches of Kaarsi. He would have devoured and then become the very thing he drew forth with the aid of his tree of Coral."

"I… see." Her expression did not change. "And now you are here to take his place."

"Not his place. My own."

"Well-spoken," she said as she rose. And if she was now suffering more or less than before her visit, she was hiding it well. "I will see you again, Prince Anyo – when you are not so busy."

"Busy?"

"Your other visitor will be here very soon and I have an offer he would likely not approve of."

She had already reached the exit when Anyo stood. "Wait. You know Lord Rokura?"

"I do." She took her lamp. "Goodnight, Your Highness."

And then Ibila was closing the door, soft footfalls fading. Anyo frowned after them. Exactly who had Thorn's mistress been? Once more, trying to bring her to mind from the time before his search was fruitless… he had simply never concerned himself with such things.

True to her word, a knock came mere moments after her departure. "Your Highness? The former Lord Rokura is here." A servant's respectful tones. Or, at least, polite tones; it was hard to say. Too long spent travelling through isolated parts, or smaller towns or foreign towns now, to pick up the exact nuances of palace parlance. *I'm sure it will come rushing back to me.*

"Excellent."

An older man wearing a dark cloak entered, his bearded

face serious as ever.

Yet, he now seemed somewhat more… free, than when Anyo had last seen him. Something about the way Rokura held himself. And while the Greyshield had always carried a resolute air, dedicated and dangerous too – those qualities had not faded. Whatever the case, it was strong enough to make an impression simply via the man's short greeting, acceptance of water and then as he seated himself opposite Anyo.

"I appreciate that you have agreed to this meeting," Anyo began. "From your report, you played in important part in protecting Iggy, and thus the realm." He lifted a small stack of pages from the low table between them. "I appreciate the grave risk you have taken by even writing these words down, for you have also saved not only considerable bloodshed in the south, but my half-brother – at the cost of my sister, I suppose. I hope Asaro is safe and perhaps even recovering?"

"If you are seeking threats, Your Highness, I cannot speak for Asaro." Rokura's words contained no venom, nor much emotion at all. The older man had simply expressed a fact, it seemed.

Anyo narrowed his eyes. "That was rather ungenerous."

"So I must seem. But even when I take your reputation into consideration, I remain wary."

Perhaps not a surprise, considering a second, very different report Anyo also had in his possession – one that appeared brimming with flimsy justifications for Rokura's exile. "My reputation?"

"As someone concerned with peace. At least, compared to the rest of your family."

"It is a reputation I mean to exceed. Starting with Takirov."

Rokura exhaled. "A fine goal, but perhaps a naïve one."

"Not the first time I've heard that." Anyo grinned. "Nor the first time I've been underestimated."

"I fear you underestimate the depth of bitterness between Nasaru and Takirov – a legendary blade will not be enough."

"Nor is a sword always the best way to peace," Anyo replied with a shrug. "But I find it hard to believe you accepted my invitation tonight just to undermine my vision for a future that offers the people if nothing so grand as peace, at least a time of less suffering."

"Fair point, lad."

"Then will you help me? I can restore your title and lands, your station and role, whatever else you ask. I can grant new purpose, if that is what you seek."

Now Rokura smiled, and it was somewhat bitter. "New purpose… Some would see my actions as untrustworthy at best. Pure treason, on the whole. Are you sure that is something you want at your side?"

"Some secrets within your report will be staying with me and me alone. And your role might well end up being in the shadows, but yes – you are still the man my father relied upon and now that you saved Asaro's life, I believe you could be someone I wish to rely upon."

The former Greyshield leant forward, his expression easing somewhat. "Considering the rumours running rife in the city, I think you are asking all who support you to enter a time of vicious turmoil before any of your dreams might come to fruition."

"I am." And not just the palace squabbles, poisonous as they would be, but Ebatru would absolutely bring an army of one size or another to the city.

"Then I will consider your offer, Your Highness," the man said as he rose.

"I appreciate that." Once more, Anyo found himself seeing someone off – though like Ibila, Rokura did not need to be escorted to the door, nor would the Greyshield need a guide on the way from the palace to wherever it was he stayed.

The meeting had gone well enough.

Yet satisfaction was thin.

Binya still loomed large in his thoughts as he moved to the window and drew the curtains open fully now. There, moonlight splashed across both the tiles and then further below, the little stone paths in the western garden, mostly leeched of colour.

Thankfully, the light did not reveal any luminous, creeping creatures.

Only, perhaps, gathering storm clouds.

Tomorrow. Tomorrow would have to be soon enough to find her – he had put it off long enough.

CHAPTER 36. – ANYO

The next morning, before he had truly commenced searching for Binya, found him barely two streets from the palace walls. There, he, Han and Katonga had stopped to speak briefly with exited folk – important, should he wish to maintain some goodwill – but even in plain clothes, riding horses without any particular trappings, it was difficult not to draw attention.

And somehow, he need not have bothered setting out, for there was Binya in her usual leathers, approaching from a cross-street, smile upon her face.

Beside Anyo, Han merely shook his head.

Katonga chuckled. "Sometimes life is blessed by a little convenience."

"You know, that's easier to believe now, compared to when we were slogging through a marsh assaulted by insects day after day," Anyo replied. "Or hanging in a steel box in the sky."

"Well said, Your Highness."

"Titles? None of that from you, old friend."

Katonga grinned, and even Han smiled before waving Anyo forward. "She isn't my first choice for an ally, but she proved herself more than once, that's for certain. Go, see what she has to say, lad. We'll be waiting."

Anyo dismounted, walking to join Binya where she waited beneath an arch of pale red stone carved with various flowers. She led him beyond to a quiet square with a dry fountain. That too, was shaped as a graceful flower with buds blooming and messages to loved ones circling the base.

No-one else stood within; they were joined only by dust and the skeletal remains of vines upon the walls.

"I am surprised but glad you found me here," he said, the words coming in place of perhaps what ought to have been a proper greeting.

She smiled. "In such a private place, or at all?"

"Both, since one of my tasks for today was to find you."

"Well, it's not difficult to plot a path to somewhere quiet when you arrive at the palace early enough to see the future king leaving."

"They say it pays to be prepared." *Trust her to be both considered in choosing a meeting place* and *one step ahead of me.* "Then, did you come to me for assurance?"

"Yes. I've made amends, as best I can, to those I disappointed before we left, and so now it is time for exactly that, Your Highness."

He grinned. "To be honest, I would have accepted an apology also."

"Oh?" She folded her arms, but she was also smiling.

"You were, of course, right about my secrets but I did not sacrifice myself." He paused. Someone else had done such a thing. "But I have a chance to live up to my oath now, and have come to remind you that I will do exactly that."

"Setting that particular moment to one side, you can still

make the same foolish mistake at another time. It's something that is within you, Anyo. Not a terrible thing, but you cannot blame me for my failure to easily banish some doubts."

"Then before that happens, Binya, join me in the struggle for change."

She unfolded her arms, resting them upon the stone as she regarded him a moment. "Are you looking for a symbol, then?"

"No." His next words did not follow at first, not until he reached out to place a hand upon hers, warmth welcome. Somehow, doing so helped. "I have wished you were by my side since you left. Not Binya the Liyrax or the symbol of Takirov, but Binya the woman."

She paused a moment, then lifted his hand and pressed it to her lips. "That was absolutely the right thing to say, Anyo – but I believe I must disappoint you."

An emptiness opened in his gut at her words. "I see."

She released his hand. "I will gladly share your bed again, should you ask, but not your life, Your Highness. You have assumed a burden that would take me away from those who depend on me, and also make me a target. I will not take that risk."

"That is fair." Something of his courtly youth lurched into his words. "And quite a gracious refusal, madam." A grin followed. "Be certain that I will make that request, too."

She chuckled. "I'm not saying that I won't help you, either. Especially if one of your first ideas is to build new homes, as we discussed, even if they are small at first."

"It is," he said with a nod. "And the Coral Trade will follow, just as soon as I deal with my brother."

Binya's cheer faded. "I have heard the rumours. They say he

is also hiring mercenaries."

"Such is the burden I have taken on, as you say. And that is not a complaint."

"It's your resolve," she said with a nod. "Something else I saw when I took on your secrets."

Anyo nearly asked her about those that remained – but to what end? Wouldn't they simply hamper his next days, weeks and years? *I have a long hill to climb, and little time to drag my doubts along behind.* Instead, it would be the nation of Nasaru that would need to be pulled after, to finally settle in a higher, better place.

To become a beacon of hope, perhaps.

Hmmm. That's getting a little ahead of myself.

She stood as if to leave but he caught her hand. "Binya. We only came as far as we did, thanks to you."

"We all struggled. Especially those two from Nokema – you're doing something for them too, aren't you?"

"As soon as they can be found, or as soon as they ask. Whichever is first."

"Good. Now, let me get back to work, Anyo."

He released her with a smile.

***

When at last he reached the palace once more, sending Han and Katonga to gather any new reports on Ebatru, and went to his old room to rest, Anyo paused with a hand upon the Solathic's hilt.

A strange woman stood within the centre of the rug.

Strange, because purple from her bare feet was bleeding into the fabric – a stain that crept toward the edges, overcoming the yellow thread.

She wore a dark robe, open enough that he could tell the rest of her skin was purple but her face was difficult to fathom… as if no matter that he was staring directly at her, all he could see were bright eyes.

And though he kept hold of the mythical weapon, it was clear that even such a blade would not harm the figure that stood before him. Clear that he should not even think for a moment of doing so.

Somehow, she was beyond even the Moon Father's all-smothering power. She was… *I do not even know how to describe this.*

Prince Anyo. Simply call me Mistress.

He nodded.

I am sure you are aware that your life from now has been gifted to you.

"Mei's brother saved us all."

She glided a little closer, and still he could not see her face clearly. **Iggy chose as much, yes. But my sisters and I are the ones you will answer to.**

Concern began to worm its way down his spine but in a distant way, somewhat removed from the current conversation, as though she were too powerful to even cause fear. "I do not understand, Mistress."

It is simple enough. In our absence, you are responsible for harmony. She reached out and her hand brushed against his chest. A purple glow answered – and then a fluttering echoed within his torso, as if flower petals were falling. It faded… but the change was permanent, there was no doubt.

"Wait." His voice was the loudest it had been since he entered the room, panic driving it up despite her presence.

"What do you mean? What did you do to me?"

Granted you a charmed, extended life to go with the hardships you will face.

He frowned. "Charmed…"

No life is endless – at least, no mortal life – and you are not invulnerable, but I have given you the tools that you might succeed in what cannot be ignored. You must use my gifts yourself, however. The absence of a guiding hand? That is the cost of the life you have been afforded by another.

The Mistress was fading.

Anyo reached up to his chest as he stepped forward, but the stern and terrifying woman was gone; the rug back to its natural yellow, the room feeling large once more, tension vanishing from his muscles.

Do not disappoint us, Beggar Pince.

***

Anyo paced away the remainder of the afternoon, having surely made deep grooves in the rug and the stone beneath. The feeling within his chest, as though petals fluttered gently down a hollow tree trunk, had returned once and not since.

A small mercy only, since a thin, purple mark now ran across his skin like a tattoo. It travelled from his heart and halfway around his torso. What purpose did it serve? Perhaps because it was a visible reminder of what had happened, it was all the more worrisome.

"I don't feel any different," he murmured.

Something he'd said aloud several times.

Whatever the case, there was nothing he could do… even if her words echoed in his memory. Charmed and extended. What exactly did that mean?

He slumped across his bed. Did it matter, for the time being?

It did, but so much was still to be done. *The more things change, the more they stay the same.*

Senoja had to be watched for an unfavourable response to…. events in Kaarsi. There was still a likely civil war to be won. Not to mention the shifting alliances within the palace itself. The mysterious Ibila would need to be better understood, and help from not only Lord Rokura and Binya, but hopefully Nuvin when he returned and perhaps even Nokema…

Delegates would be sent upon the morrow.

There was even a letter from the Royal Sorcerers upon his desk regarding clean up, use, and possible distribution of the ruined Coral Tree.

Above such concerns stood Asaro Itonye. More immediate still, Chiotta.

With whom would she throw her lot?

He had to smile. Hardly the right question. *A better question is exactly what steps has she already taken for herself?*

All had to be dealt with, no matter that one of the Fates had done something to him. And the first step was to deal with the evening. Selecting the proper attire for the Beggar Prince's official return to court, followed by the much-anticipated meeting with his younger sister.

He sighed as he rose, then strode for the bathtub where it stood on horned feet in an adjoining room. "I hope you're doing the right thing, Chi."

Because the kingdom is mine now.

CHAPTER 37. – ROKURA

Rokura quickened his step on the way back from the palace, boots echoing along the empty side street. For now, he had not kept his word. Isetta's message would not be delivered, not until he spent a little more time to take Anyo's measure. *After all, this is a time for prudence.*

Although, not for everyone.

Not even himself. Especially considering his decision to write the report he did... And the new king, should Anyo hold on to power, had to act swiftly on several fronts also.

Cobbles gleamed beneath the faintest of rain and the ornate, flower-like streetlamps took on an ethereal quality – something the artisan might not have intended. So too, the paintings found upon the Grand Gallery's exterior walls as he passed.

But on the third painting, this of a fawn in a glade, there was a more curious purple tint. He slowed. The figure was not in fact a fawn, but a woman whose robes could have been made from petals...

The Mistress of Obsidian?

Rokura stopped and found himself at eye-level with the

Mistress – the sound of water striking stone echoed in the street, so loud that it seemed to have stopped everything.

And it had!

Even beads of water hung frozen in the air. Nearby lamps did not flicker and a passing carriage sat within the intersection, the legs of each horse lifted...

Rokura. Will you hear my offer?

"Mistress. I am surprised to speak with you once more."

Doubtless.

Clearly, she was not planning to elaborate. And while she was a being of vast power that even now weighed upon him, before hearing her offer Rokura had a question to ask – a question he was yet to discover an answer for. "Did you keep your promise?"

I do not care for your doubt. Should you refer to Iggy, then he chose not to receive that which he sought. Instead, my Sisters and I saved victims of the Moon Father, as per Iggy's request.

"Iggy..." Such a thing was not unlike the young man, but where did that leave the lad? And did it mean that somehow, Iggy had put a stop to the Moon Father? Where was he? Had he found his sister at least?

Nothing prevents you from seeking Iggy after this meeting, should you wish. A frown creased her face now, and something unseen clamped itself across his mouth – while it did not stop him breathing, he could not speak to object. **Hear me. I offer you a future where you will assuredly make a difference to the lives of those around you, to your nation. It will not be a future free of hardship, should you accept. Either way, responsibility for harmony passes from us, now.**

The block upon his voice lifted then, but in a way, such a

thing did not help at all. "Mistress… Are you telling me there is another threat?"

There will always be another threat.

A patient answer to a foolish question, perhaps. But she was offering something not dissimilar to what Prince Anyo had put forward during their meeting. *And I cannot lie to myself with some half-hearted refusal.* "If I am given the chance to face those threats, I would understand more."

At last, the Mistress smiled. **Your nobility cannot be hidden by a change of cloak, I see.**

"Thank you for the compliment." And coming from her, it was high praise. "Do you need to… change me to better face whatever is to come?"

Subtly, and not in a way that you will find disagreeable. She reached out before he could actually accept her offer, hand pressed against his heart. Within, it seemed as though a clear bell chimed.

But the sensation did not linger.

And the Mistress was already fading back into the artwork, purple vanishing along with her bright gaze.

All around, the city returned to movement; soft rain falling, the carriage rattling by. Rokura frowned as he turned from the painting – once more a fawn – and strode along the street. What exactly had she done? *And what must we face in the future?*

Above all, however, what of Iggy? Whatever the Mistress had changed within him, it obviously wasn't intended to stop him seeking out Iggy in some way. Hopefully, sooner rather than later.

On Rokura strode, passing a beggar huddled against the wall, the man's head wrapped in bandages. On again toward a squat, darkened building that appeared not unlike a prison. And so it would have been, but the old king changed his mind and the stony place became an inn.

Chiefly used by injured soldiers close to full recovery, the inn was more affordable than many other places in the Autumn City. And luckily, the young attendant had not recognised him, despite previous visits.

Once inside, Rokura strode to the room where he'd left Asaro. He took a moment to shake the dew from his cloak at the door.

The bell within him chimed again, faint and something only he could hear presumably, but somehow, it was a reassuring sound, for all its unnaturalness. He unlocked the door and entered a simple room. The inn provided only a single bed and no natural light fell upon its stone walls, but aside from its fair price, the other desirable feature was its distance from prying eyes.

Asaro remained seated upon the thin blankets, legs crossed beneath him. He was still writing in the small journal, and he looked up as Rokura returned, expression quite expectant. "What did you learn?"

He did not answer at once. Perhaps far too much had been learnt.

"Is something wrong?" Asaro asked.

"No," Rokura said as he handed over street food wrapped in broad leaves that he had purchased earlier. It was not much, but until he chose to return to the king's service – as it seemed he might well do – such was all that could be afforded. "Prince Anyo may well prove to be someone worth following."

"I see."

Had there been a note of discontent? *Did I actually pay attention to his answer?* "Does that disappoint you, lad?"

Asaro lowered his quill. "No. But it might leave me with a different purpose, and I have not considered it fully. Actually, I haven't fully considered very many futures at all, to be honest. Less so, after being abducted."

"I could just as easily take you home as to the palace."

"Something tells me I can achieve more from Omaila, no matter my specific role in the royal household."

"It may be so, yes."

"What about Isetta's package?" Asaro asked around a mouthful, the scent of buttery, toasted bread filling the room.

Rokura removed the small box, wrapped in layers of green and yellow ribbon, and set it within the palm of his hand. The voyage home to Omaila had certainly been made longer by his doubts. Would handing it over create more trouble than failing to do so?

"You kept it, then."

Rokukra nodded. "For now. I need to think a little longer – it is too dangerous for me to rush."

"All that time on the sea wasn't enough?"

"Not at all, lad."

CHAPTER 38. – ROKURA

It was early enough that few people walked the streets beneath a slowly brightening sky, caught somewhere between black and grey. A gentle breeze swept down, warmer than expected, urging dry leaves along gutters.

On the surface, a pleasant morning.

Even if Asaro had grumbled a little at being roused from sleep, or that the promises of the Mistress continued to weigh upon Rokura's mind. Not only had she changed him in some way, but she promised more turmoil.

Where? And for whom exactly?

The looming possibility of civil strife was the obvious candidate, but was her warning really aimed at something with such a long list of historical precedent? War with Senoja would be on the same list. *But for something like another Moon Father, will she and her sisters really leave us?*

Although, when it came to precedent, a world without gods to guide it was hardly a unique thing either. *We've been alone before, and we will do so again.*

"Even in this light, it is far larger than I imagined," Asaro said from where he walked beside Rokura.

"You didn't get a good glimpse before?"

"Not precisely," he replied. "My mind was occupied with various disappointments."

"Revenge?"

He shrugged. "Among other things, but I can take revenge in more ways than one – I can become something he never wanted for me."

Rokura glanced down at him. "Thinking of the crown?"

"No." Asaro's answer held no trace of hesitation. "I will simply live a happy and useful life – after I've helped the other bastards."

Quite the mature response.

Ahead, a figure detached itself from one of the walls; it seemed to be the same beggar from last night, quite tall, his head wrapped in bandages. And while at first, the beggar approached Rokura with bowl in hand, the man's steps quickly turned to Asaro…

… and the city froze once more, a faint bell chiming as it did.

In the silent world of stillness that remained, the glint of a dagger in the man's other hand became clear, outlined by a thin flame of white. Yet it did not move; nothing was moving.

Except me.

Was this what the Mistress had promised when she told him he had been changed? If so, it could prove troubling… considering he did not know how to restore the flow of moments.

But the threat was undeniable.

Rokura drew near – only to stumble to a halt.

Up close, the beggar was all-too-familiar, even with his face half-concealed by bandages.

Edazol!

However his old mentor managed it, Edazol had followed across the sea and into the city, stalking his prey. And now, in the dark of the early morning, he obviously planned to finish what Princess Kiteka started back in Viareya.

But what exactly can I do here? Rokura paused.

Would striking Edazol have any effect, one way or another? Would it stop the attack – providing time could be restored at a moment of his choosing? *What if I have a limit to how long I can be here?* Rokura reached out to touch Edazol's shoulder. Cold and hard as stone. *So I'll merely break my own hand. Or weapon.*

And it was the weapon that cried for attention in the frozen world, wasn't it?

Meaning that is my only clue.

Rokura drew his own blade and lifted it, glancing back to Asaro. The young man wore an expression of mild concern where he stood, not so close as to be in danger. At least, depending on what happened next. *But you cannot stay here forever.* Still Rokura hesitated, yet an action had to be taken.

Hopefully, striking the knife would… break the stillness, somehow.

He swung down – hard enough – and white sparks flew. The dagger skittered across the stones as motion returned to the world.

Edazol stumbled forward, thumping into Rokura. Yet Rokura was ready for the possibility. He dropped his shoulder, bent his knees and surged upright, casting the lighter man into the air.

Defenceless, Edazol crashed to the stones with a shout, bandage spiralling free.

There was no time to lose the advantage. Rokura pounced upon the Greyshield, knees crashing into his mentor's chest, his own blade flashing up to rest against the man's throat. Edazol's eyes were wide as he no doubt struggled to comprehend what had just happened.

"What are you doing?" Asaro cried from behind.

"Foiling an assassination attempt. See his dagger over there?" Yet Rokura had not taken his eyes from his old master. "Do you wish to live, Edazol?"

Edazol's eyes narrowed. "What?"

"I offer mercy. Take it and I will turn you over to the new king. Depending on what you have to say, he may spare your life."

"A traitor to the end, I see." Edazol's arm twitched as he spoke. "You disappoint –"

Rokura shoved his blade down. Blood bloomed but he did not stop there, whipping the edge across Edazol's throat and rising with a frown. Dark bubbles rose as the man clutched at his throat, but life was vanishing from his eyes, his limbs weakening so, so swiftly.

A second knife clinked against the street, resting beside Edazol's hand.

Asaro joined Rokura and the lad was breathing a little hard. "Are you sure he meant to attack me?"

"I have no doubt."

"Then… thank you for saving my life once more." Asaro shook his head, swallowing. "I didn't even see him as a threat."

Rokura knelt to use Edazol's cloak to wipe blood from his blade, something that was becoming an all-too-familiar action. "Do not be hard on yourself." *I was a little slow myself.* Without the mysterious gift from the Mistress, how different might the attack gone? Few were as fast as Edazol had been. A little knot of guilt tightened within his chest.

"Do we wait for someone to come? Guards?" Asaro asked.

Once, the Greyshield's code would have had him do so, after what amounted to an Execution, especially that of a fellow Greyshield. But the word 'fellow' no longer applied to Edazol. To any Greyshield.

"No."

"Well…"

Rokura gestured to the gleaming palace before sheathing his weapon. "We will send someone when we reach the gates, but for now it is time for you to take a step toward that happy and useful life you mentioned before."

CHAPTER 39. – MEI

Mamalo joined her upon the bench with a sharp hiss of pain.

"You didn't hurt yourself again, did you?" she asked without looking from the road, reins in hand. While it was easy enough to drive the wagon along such well-maintained stone, especially with the horse knowing exactly what to do, it was hardly a task she had undertaken so many times that it had suddenly became second nature.

And it was far more difficult than riding the light.

"No, thankfully." Something about his tone of voice seemed unusual. "It still hurts, is all."

She glanced at him, then back to the road. He had not leant down to massage his foot, nor was his expression twisted in pain. Instead, he stared toward the tree line, or perhaps just above at the distant blue sky and its wisp of cloud.

"Are you worried about something? Bandits?" she asked. "Negotiations when we reach Anikaja?"

"No, not truly."

"The others? I'm sure Nilo and Nata will be fine. After what you three already went through, returning home shouldn't be so much trouble, surely? And it sounds like that Lio owes you all."

"No, I agree with you there."

She frowned. "Then, is it Iggy? He'll meet us as soon as –"

"I believe your brother, Mei. But since I'm doing such a poor job of hiding my concerns, let me ask you instead. Are you sure?"

Her grip on the leather loosened. "You kept your word and I'm keeping mine. I'll help you with your negotiations."

He chuckled. "You know that's not what I'm asking. Are you sure about this instead of returning home."

"I am."

Mei added nothing more; she had already made her decision. Home was not in the village. Not anymore.

Mamalo did not press her and by the time they passed beneath the branches, it was time to set up camp. He soon had a fire going, while Mei gathered more fuel from beside the nearby road. The earth remained mostly free of undergrowth, since the woods were made up of plentiful, visible root systems. They were starkly pale in the firelight where they clung to the rocky earth. In places, the roots pushed through with greying, stringy leaves.

Yet an almost golden fruit hung from the branches above, berries that grew in little clumps of three. Supposedly quite poisonous, according to Mamalo.

"We might do well to harvest some in any event," he said from where he was unpacking cooking utensils. "Good for making medicine. Just be careful not to break the skin."

Mei reached up and used her belt knife to cut some free, making a small pile before Mamalo nodded. "I'd help myself, you know."

"It's fine. You earned that injury trying to find me, and I appreciate it."

"Well, if I'd…" He trailed off at the sound of hooves echoing through the wood.

Mei lowered the pile of berries. Mamalo was already on his feet, concern glittering in his gaze. "Best be ready."

Without much in the way of sunlight to call upon, Mei readied herself to attack with a more familiar psychic blast – if needed.

But the figures who slowed to approach the camp did so without ill intent; even though one was a warrior, dressed in pale breastplate with blue gauze, a silver circlet upon her brow. The woman's bow was not in hand and her thin blade remained sheathed. Instead, the soldier helped the other rider from her mount – this woman younger, eyes a little wide. Her features were softer than the warrior's, blonde hair almost white and a silken robe of ivory peeked from beneath her cloak. *Not common travelling garb, unless travelling by carriage, perhaps.*

"Forgive us, travellers, but might we share your fire this evening?" The young woman, who may have been a noble or at least quite wealthy, spoke fair Nasaru.

Even without Mei's earring to help, her ability to read the emotions and thoughts of the visitors was enough – it had certainly only grown stronger in the aftermath of the Moon Father. And while the request from the woman – she *was* a noble – had been undercut with exhaustion and concern, the thoughts of the warrior were far louder. Those pressed against Mei's very temples. Suspicion. That, and a desperation to flee the capital.

But nothing which suggested either woman meant them

ill will.

And it seemed Mamalo had come to a similar conclusion as he made introductions and bade them to sit. Knowing the former Greyshield, he was probably seeking information as much as displaying kindness.

"I see you are merchants," the noble said. For the moment, she had not introduced herself and her protector had not spoken at all.

"We are," Mamalo replied. "Perhaps you could share something of what lies ahead?"

"Of course." Though it took her a moment to continue and she offered no name. "There is some unrest in Anikaja, but nothing that will trouble you in the markets."

"Oh?"

The warrior placed a hand upon the noblewoman's arm but did not speak. The younger woman nodded. "To allay your fears, Mamalo, perhaps especially *not* for a Nasaru merchant with a local guide," she said, finishing with a look across to Mei.

"That is a relief to hear," Mei replied, keeping her thoughts interwoven with her words. Something she had been doing for such a long time without thinking, it was only now that she tried to make sure… and couldn't remember, had she spoken in Nasaru or Senoja?

"Yes." The noblewoman's answer held a little sadness.

And though Mamalo asked again across the course of the evening, little else was learnt. Something had happened in the capital, connected no doubt to the emperor, but once they had eaten and sought their beds, Mei was none the wiser.

Encouragingly, if nothing else, the travellers seemed to

accept her as Senoja.

She turned upon her bedroll, closed her eyes and tried to put the mystery out of her mind despite the fact that the travellers were mere paces away, on the other side of the fire.

By morning, the two women had gone.

Mei circled the campsite with a frown, waiting for the sun to penetrate the pale trees and give her that extra bit of energy for the day ahead. "Did you hear them?"

"I did," Mamalo replied as he began to strike his tent, still moving gingerly. "It seemed better to let them leave."

"I suppose you're right."

"Curious?"

She spread her hands. "Aren't you?"

"A little." He paused, resting the tent pole across his knees. "But ignorance may work in our favour, if we are questioned in the capital."

"Then, the noblewoman *was* fleeing something serious?"

"We won't know for certain, but it seemed that way." He ran a hand through his hair. "But to be honest, she had quite a high-ranking soldier with her. She's going to be well cared for."

"Good." Mei moved to the carriage, rummaging around for water to douse the fire.

"I'm more concerned about Iggy, right now," he said.

"I'll check on him again, soon. He'll join us. He just needs time to himself."

"He's earned whatever he needs, Mei. I just want to prepare him for the scrutiny he'll be under in the capital."

She smiled to herself as she lifted one of the smaller barrels. "He might surprise us both, you know."

CHAPTER 40. – IGGY

He hovered just beyond the walls of Hiila, waiting for the sun to finish sinking into the plain – that, and for a suitable wagon, carriage or party of travellers to use for cover.

In the darkness within the walls, he could keep to the shadows, keep his hood raised and avoid everyone and at least that way, still get close enough to… to what? *Something I can still only imagine?*

Iggy placed a hand upon his chest where he sat beneath the branches. The Sisters were gone. It had been painless, and even the memory of the weight he had carried vanished too, but at the same time, not a single word from Nuka, or even the Mistress, since making his choice.

Bitterness did linger.

But it was not a choice he would change… it simply meant that he would have to find another way to win a new life.

Iggy, can you hear me? Mei, her voice reaching him from some distance.

I can. I don't think we'll have trouble now, no matter how far apart we are.

It seemed she smiled. *That's something. Is Zeana somewhere safe?*

Yes. And I'll check on them when they're ready.

Good. Are you joining us now?

Soon.

There's not a lot of sunlight left. We'll reach Anikaja around noon, tomorrow.

A carriage rumbled by, vibrations finding him where he waited, wheels slowing as it neared the sturdy gates. Iggy pushed himself from his log and started walking. *That might be better.*

Whenever you're ready – just stay safe.

I will. You too, Mei.

Of all the changes to come about after leaving Nokema, perhaps the best one was that he would soon be able to travel with his sister, together, free from all the suspicion and expectations of home. It actually added a little spring to his step as he neared the gate.

But before rejoining Mei, there was something to test.

And something to remember.

Providing everything worked out. Based on knowledge he'd been able to steal from Thorn, there shouldn't be much doubt, but a true trial had to be undertaken. And so he picked up his pace, and as the guards strode from the gate house in their pale armour and gauze, all grey but presumably one colour or another, Iggy drew close.

As he did, he used his gift not to force something away, not to strike out, but to *suggest*.

And just like Thorn must have done so many times, Iggy found the minds of the guards. Their concerns regarding the carriage were perfunctory. Instead, they were keen to return to their game of dice and dry wine.

Which only made it easier to suggest to the pair that he

belonged. That he was nothing to glance at more than once. And even then, just a wave and a grunt would suffice…

Iggy nearly faltered when one of the soldiers did exactly as expected.

A rush of success fuelled his steps as he hurried across stone toward the nearest alley. It rested right beside an inn, light and glimpses of laughing faces clear through the windows. The side street not only kept him hidden when it came to passersby, but allowed him to consider his next test.

Doubtless, the darkness had helped at the gate. The distraction of a carriage to be searched, the impatience of the guards, perhaps his own smaller, non-threatening stature… *Even my skin probably helped at least a little.*

Would everything be so easy in the harsh light of day?

Somewhere beyond Senoja?

Whatever the result during daylight, another trial needed to be completed at night. And then, a final attempt under lamplight. He glanced to the mouth of the alley, where a group of men and women tumbled forth.

Perhaps the test would be better undertaken in a quieter inn. But either way, he would master the technique before rejoining Mei.

He left the alley and strode along, keeping away from the brighter lights and other people, trying to exude a general sense that he was not worth looking at, and soon reaching a section of Hiila with polished boards. A calmer place.

And there, at the first inn he chose, practically shouting at anyone inside with his mind about just how normal he was, he found no free rooms to rent. But nor did he receive odd looks from the woman he spoke with, at least.

An equally serene place was not so far away, similar picture of a bed hanging above its door.

Inside the common room, he sent out another suggestion that covered the half dozen patrons at their meals. And once more, no-one paid him much attention at all. *This is perfect.*

He approached the barkeeper next, a small man with an impressively plaited beard. Here, Iggy sent not only the sense that he belonged, but that he was speaking aloud. *A room and water, please.*

"Not a problem." The man turned back to retrieve a key from within a cabinet.

Thank you.

But when the innkeeper placed the room key upon the polished counter, scooping up the coins Iggy offered – all of them – the man hesitated, eyes narrowing. "A moment, lad. Are you unwell?"

No. Why?

"Something about your face…"

Iggy pushed a little harder, repeating the idea that he belonged. *Nothing about me is out of place. My face is normal. I just look a little tired, is all.*

The innkeeper shrugged. "My mistake, that was a little rude of me. Please, enjoy your night."

I will, thank you.

Iggy took the key and headed down a short corridor to a row of rooms. Not unlike the building itself, and others within Senoja, small potted plants stood by the doors. His plant bloomed in the shape of little bells, and he paused to take one between his fingers, soft and smooth.

Almost let myself believe I'd be able to understand the scent of a flower.

Which was a lie.

Not almost. He *had* let himself believe.

Foolish of me. He turned the key in its lock, entered the room and let his cloak drop to the floor before collapsing onto the big bed. The sharp sting of a dream denied was swirling up again, tempering the triumph from his successes since entering the small city.

Iggy rolled onto his side, pulling his knees up toward his chest and despite being alone, he fought back the urge to rock in place, like a child. Weariness came upon the heels of the burst of grief. Due to the use of his power in a new manner? Whatever the cause, the growing lethargy promised a certain amount of oblivion, at least.

From the darkness came instead, a glowing field of flames…

… and he walked among them, each little flame standing in place of a petal. He was drawn immediately to the centre, where there waited a patient figure.

She was short, but no child considering the sense of age that washed over Iggy, wearing a shapeless smock and bracelets upon her wrists. But when he reached her, he could not confirm whether she was elderly, as her face was difficult to really understand. Only her eyes were clear, kind and bright.

Nuka?

Of course, Iggy. But we have to hurry now, I'm not supposed to be doing this.

Do you mean visit? He hastened to her side, and now her smile was visible, long hair seeming to breathe where it fell to her shoulders. She reached across to cup his cheek.

No. I mean what I am going to do. It is against long-standing covenants. **She shrugged.** But then, I wrote them with my sisters, so why shouldn't I?

I don't understand, Nuka.

I'm saying that I'm going to break one for you now.

Tension grew. *Wait, I don't want you to suffer because of me.*

You forget what I am, Iggy – so worry not. And I want you to think about yourself, instead. It is time to put your life first. **She lifted her free hand to take his other cheek, then leant in close enough that her lips brushed his forehead.** Now, go and sleep again. When you wake, you will have a face. Your face, just as you deserve.

I…

Was it true?

There was no reason for her to lie – she and her Sisters already had what they longed for, didn't they? There would be no way it could be a lie, she was telling the truth, wasn't she?

Your face is not my only gift, but you will have to use them without my guidance from now on. It will not be easy, but you are strong enough.

Darkness was returning with a swiftness that smothered even his shock, but it seemed that somehow, even as Nuka and her field disappeared, that he was able to smile.

CHAPTER 41. – MEI

"I hate to bring it up again, but I want you to humour me once more, Mei."

Mamalo was regarding her with some sternness where they rode upon the carriage, reins in one hand and a flask of water in the other.

The same woods were rolling by on either side, but somewhere beyond the screen of white trunks, grey leaves and clumps of yellow berries, came the echo of human activity: the thud of axes and raised voices. They were nearing the capital, and Mei could not deny an excitement growing within. It was mixed with nerves – could she really negotiate properly?

Either way, it was hard to believe she was actually going to see Anikaja.

Hard to believe that she was finally travelling without being chased, or held prisoner.

Without being exhausted. Or desperate to stop a decaying god from returning to destroy everything and everyone, too.

"I'm happy with my choice. Is that so hard to believe?"

"Well… yes. When we found you on that beach – or actually, when you found us and explained everything, I felt quite profound relief. And it struck me, isn't there someone back home who deserves to feel that?"

Mamalo was right… there was at least one person, but Arun would survive. As would the rest of the village; they had each other. And they didn't really know the danger she'd faced either. *They will manage without me.* "Hearing that you were worried is enough."

He rubbed his temples then, though he smiled too. "Then, I've got one last thing to try. An appeal to a petty emotion, perhaps."

"Very well."

"Isn't there a part of you that wants to go back, at least one day – if for no other reason than to show them what you've done? That they were wrong about Iggy?"

Mei sighed, in part because she'd already had the same conversation with herself, and in part because there was a fragment of her that *did* want exactly that. *Especially Mother.* And perhaps, to be sure her aunt had survived… But once again, her decision had been made. "Mamalo, is there some reason *you* want me to go back one day?"

He chuckled. "When you put it that way, maybe there is."

"Then tell me."

"Regret, that is all. Maybe I don't want you to regret something like that, because I know how it feels."

"Oh."

"It was quite a long time ago." He drank from the flask. "And to be honest, I'm pushing too much. I mean, just because I'm convinced something was right for me, doesn't mean it's right for someone else."

Mei nodded. "Then you'll accept my answer now?"

"Of course. Just tell me if you want company, if you do decide to go back."

"I will," she said, and trailed off.

Between one blink and the next, Mamalo had disappeared – replaced by a woman wearing a white robe and veil, leaving naught but a pair of bright eyes discernible.

But a sense of immeasurable knowledge and power was contained in the woman's gaze, leaving no room for doubt as to who now sat across from her. The only question was which of the three Fates… or perhaps, it did not matter?

Mei. I have come with an offer. One which I urge you to accept in our absence.

"May I ask, why come to me?"

Did she smile in response? Impossible to be sure, for the woman's face was difficult to read, even aside from the veil. You are already blessed, certainly. But it will not be enough for the trials ahead. If you accept, you will be changed, giving you the means to change that around you.

"Will I be able to help Iggy?"

Many others, but not your brother.

Somehow, not surprising – but still disappointing. "And I must decide now."

A nod.

"You said 'in your absence'. Where are you going?"

Elsewhere. It is time to choose, Mei of Nokema. Will you stand with the other heroes?

"I will."

A fine choice. I suspect you will do so without my urging, but do use your gifts wisely.

And then Mamalo was sitting beside her once more, taking

another drink of water before glancing to the road ahead.

Mei opened her mouth to tell him… but stopped. What was there to share? She did not know what had been done, did not know what it meant. What new means did she have to face future problems? For now, there was little to explain… even the implication that a new threat would rise remained vague and undefined.

So I might as well just wait and see?

No sooner had she finished the thought, when something swelled within her chest, a joyous rhythm of hooves upon an open plain… but it faded quickly.

Another mystery.

"There's someone up ahead," Mamalo said, squinting a little. "Hopefully we can ask them for information about the capital; I've never seen so few travellers on a road."

Mei followed his gaze. The figure was some distance away, too hard to see clearly. But something about him seemed familiar… dark hair and dark cloak, the young man's face not very distinct yet, but still, why did it seem she knew him?

He hadn't approached, but was he smiling, blue eyes twinkling with perhaps a hint of mischief even?

The horses drew them closer and closer until she stood in her seat.

Mamalo started. "Mei?"

"I think…" She let her mind do the last of the seeking – and then she was leaping down to sprint along the road, laughing as she did.

EPILOGUE – CINDER

When Cinder hit the bottom he was still alive.

The word 'hit' was probably too strong in a way; for it seemed that after a time – a long time or a very long time, or both – Cinder was simply no longer falling. But he was still, so that would have to mean the bottom.

Flawless logic on my part.

In the darkness of wherever he sat, there was a little light – the blade of his stolen dagger; just enough to give him a sense of… what? Hope? *Too strong.* Far too strong for what he felt, especially when the light of the blade revealed plenty of pale mist now clinging to his body.

Or growing *from my body.*

There was no pain. No sensation at all.

Just a muting of the senses. A warmth, a calmness and a vast shadow waiting beyond the tiny borders of his blade.

Cinder didn't rise or try to move. *Best not to disrupt the peace.* Somehow, down wherever he was, nothing much seemed urgent. Countless events were happening somewhere and probably important things among them, but the tendrils themselves were aware just enough to urge him away from worry.

That for now, all he had to do was wait and watch.

Not to sleep, but to save his strength for what was coming. Something that could be felt across every ley line throughout the lands, but which could not be measured. Something that was eager to taste all of what had grown and lived while it travelled home at last.

ACKNOWLEDGMENTS

To each and everyone who supported this trilogy on Kickstarter, thank you so much, these books are for you.

It's been a long wait - but without everyone below, the wait would have gone on and on and there would have been absolutely *zero chance* that all three books would have been released together, so thank you again!

Heiko Koenig ~ Vitor Publishing ~ Jeff Lewis ~ Daryl Parat ~ Jesper Pettersen ~ Larry Couch ~ Supreme Emperor Ben Mariner ~ The Creative Fund by BackerKit ~ Stephen Ballentine ~ Esapekka Eriksson ~ John Idlor ~ David Lars Chamberlain ~ Robin Hill ~ Virginia McClain ~ Señor Neo ~ John Mackie ~ Jason Cordero ~ Richard Bunting ~ Debbie Phillips ~ Jason ~ L.M. Lacee ~ William C. Tracy ~ Erin Himrod ~ C.Wilson ~ Sven Lugar ~ Ian Linford ~ Monica Elida Forssell ~ Astridd ~ Technewszone.com ~ Samantha Landstrom ~ Anne Walker ~ Cheryl Linford ~ Zac ~ Shirley

S ~ Richard Novak ~ nny ~ Aramanth Dawe ~ Thomas Polk ~ Maddalena Tarallo ~ Donna ~ Mitchell S. ~ Trava Buono ~ Lee Dunning ~ Levid José de Jesús Montes Sánchez ~ Scott Freisthler ~ Peter & Andy ~ Fritha Blackwood ~ Leo Collis ~ Jamie-Lee Graafmans ~ Michaela Miles ~ Belinda Mellor ~ Katherine Shipman ~ Patty Jansen ~ Jessica Ward ~ Jazmine Baldwin ~ C. Gockel ~ Sven Grams ~ Matthian ~ Rhianne R. ~ Blade ~ Emma Adams ~ C.Niehot ~ Becky James ~ sabrinaweb71 ~ Tony and Ben Muzi ~ Joe Monson ~ Tao Wong ~ Zee ~ Ellen Pilcher ~ Jesper Pettersen ~ Virginia McClain ~ Award-Winning Author Wendy Scott

I am also once again in debt to Brooke! And to Rebekah at Vivid Covers for the amazing set of covers that not only showcase the main cast, but strike the perfect mood.

I must also thank Amanda at Phoenix Editing for always going beyond what I ask (especially with Volume 3!) and also David at David Schembri Studios for the formatting – I know I gave him some extra work with the range of fonts!

Ashley Capes

A NOTE FROM ASHLEY

Hello! I hope you enjoyed *Stars Burning* and thank you for reading.

If you could help me out by leaving an honest review of the book at your place of purchase, that would be fantastic! Long or short, bad or good, it all helps.

As all three volumes of the Exiles Trilogy were released together, you can already sample or purchase *Exiles: Volume 3 (Stars Burning)* at your retailer of choice!

AND if you'd like to sign up to my newsletter (https://www.subscribepage.com/b5w1k0) you'll be the first to know when future Exiles books are released. You'll also have first access to preview chapters and pre-release editions of my other stories, in addition to being automatically added into the draw for giveaways.

Ashley

www.ir.gramcontent.com/pod-product-compliance
Lightning Source LLC
Chambersburg PA
CBHW020402120726
47904CB00002B/666